By The Same Author

The Birthday Visitor
The Dancing Kettle
The Forever Christmas Tree
Journey to Topaz
The Magic Listening Cap
The Promised Year
The Rooster Who Understood Japanese
Samurai of Gold Hill
Sumi and the Goat and the Tokyo Express
Sumi's Prize

Journey
Home

Journey Home

YOSHIKO UCHIDA

illustrated by CHARLES ROBINSON

Macmillan/McGraw-Hill School Publishing Company
New York ▪ Chicago ▪ Columbus

For information regarding permission, write to Margaret K.
McElderry Books, Macmillan Publishing Company, 866 Third
Avenue, New York, NY 10022.

This edition is reprinted by arrangement with Margaret K.
McElderry Books, an imprint of Macmillan Publishing Company.

Macmillan/McGraw-Hill School Division
10 Union Square East
New York, New York 10003

Printed in the United States of America

ISBN 0-02-179528-2 / 6, L.12A

3 4 5 6 7 8 9 WES 99 98 97 96 95 94 93

For Shizuo, Kay and Michi

Journey
Home

I CAN'T SEE, YUKI THOUGHT FRANTICALLY. I CAN'T BREATHE. The screaming desert wind flung its white powdery sand in her face, stifling her and wrapping her up in a smothering cocoon of sand so fine it was like dust. It blinded her and choked her and made her gag as she opened her mouth to cry out.

The black tar-papered barracks on either side of the road had vanished behind the swirling dust, and Yuki was all alone in an eerie, unreal world where nothing existed except the shrieking wind and the great choking clouds of dust. Yuki stumbled on, doubled over, pushing hard against the wind, gasping as she felt the sting of sand and pebbles against her legs.

Suppose she never got back to her barrack? Suppose the wind simply picked her up and flung her out beyond the barbed wire fence into the desert? Suppose no one ever found her dried, wind-blown body out there in the sagebrush?

A cry of terror swelled up inside her. "Mama! Papa! Help me!"

The sound of her own scream woke her up. Yuki's heart was pounding. Her damp fists were clenched tight. Her face was wet with tears.

For several minutes she couldn't believe it was only a nightmare. It had all seemed so real, she could almost taste the flat, powdery dust in her mouth. She had been back in the Utah desert, living with Mama and Papa and her big brother, Ken, in Topaz, one of the World War II concentration camps where all the Japanese of the West Coast had been sent by the government.

Yuki shuddered and blinked hard, trying to see where she really was. Was she back in the small crowded barrack room where their four army cots were separated by army blankets strung on ropes? Would she have to wake Mama and ask her to bring the flashlight and go out to the latrine with her because she was too scared to go alone? Would she have to rush from toilet to toilet to find one that wasn't filled with filth because the water had stopped running?

Yuki gathered herself up into a small ball and hugged her knees. Gradually, slowly, she left the strange world of dreams and nightmares and knew she was safe in her room in the apartment in Salt Lake City, which the minister of the Japanese church had found for them. And he'd told them not to worry because the landlady, Mrs. Henley, didn't mind their being Japanese.

For a few moments Yuki remembered again the awful fear that had consumed her those last weeks in Topaz when Papa had been threatened by the small gang of agitators. They had turned their anger at being in camp against anyone who, like Papa, worked with the administration to keep the camp running smoothly. And finally, one night, they had thrown a stink bomb into their barrack room. After that both Mama and Papa knew it was no longer safe to remain in camp, even though they wanted to stay and do whatever they could to help their people.

"Your family has already spent almost a year in camp," the director had said to Papa. "I think it's time now that you left."

He had secured special clearance for them to leave, and they had gone to Salt Lake City as soon as possible. Now they were safe outside the camp, and there was no more barbed wire fence to keep them from going anywhere they wanted to go.

Yuki took a deep breath and wiped her nose with the corner of the sheet. Mama wouldn't like her doing that, but she was still too shaky to get out of bed. She stared into the darkness until she could make out the familiar things in her room: the big, carved-oak chest of drawers that Mrs. Henley's great-grandfather had built, the small, chintz-covered armchair that was Yuki's favorite chair in the whole apartment, and the large gold frame on the wall with the watercolor scene of sailboats in a sunny harbor.

Yes, everything was all there. It was all right. She

5

was safe, and she needn't ever worry again about being blown into the desert to turn into a heap of sunbleached bones.

But her best friend, Emi Kurihara, wasn't safe, Yuki reminded herself. Emi and her grandma had been their neighbors in camp, and they were still out there in that awful desert with its duststorms and scorpions and the guard towers and the fence.

"You'd just better hurry up and come on out," Yuki said now to Emi.

Yuki often carried on conversations with people who were hundreds of miles away, because she felt if she just concentrated hard enough the message from her brain would somehow reach theirs, no matter where they were. It was most convenient, because she could talk to Emi in Topaz, or to her brother fighting in Italy with the 442nd Regimental Combat Team, or even to her old friend Mrs. Jamieson back home in Berkeley, California. And she always had the feeling that somehow each of them got her messages.

"Don't worry," she continued to Emi. "Papa will help you and your grandma get out of camp. He said he would."

If he promised, Yuki knew he'd try. With that reassuring thought, she suddenly sat up in bed. She was famished, and she began to think about juicy hamburgers and french fries and chocolate milk shakes.

Her stomach gurgled noisily as she pulled on her bathrobe and slid into her slippers. She walked carefully toward the kitchen, giant-stepping over the boards that squeaked so she wouldn't awaken Mrs. Henley or her invalid husband or their two Siamese cats downstairs. Mrs. Henley had already warned Yuki that she was a light sleeper and could hear every night sound in the entire house.

The kitchen still smelled faintly of chicken and soy sauce, and Yuki wished she hadn't eaten the last piece at supper so there would have been some left for her now. She stared into the cold whiteness of the refrigerator and contemplated the brown paper bag with her lunch for tomorrow.

"Should I?" she asked herself.

"I should," she answered. What was wrong with putting half the baloney sandwich in her stomach right now when she was starving, instead of leaving it for tomorrow.

She sat down at the table and quickly undid the wax paper wrapping, surprised at all the noise it made in the silent kitchen.

She had just taken a bite when she heard the creak of the floor in the hallway. Yuki groaned softly. Now Mrs. Henley would probably pop out of bed and stay up the rest of the night with her cats. Then tomorrow she'd tell Yuki she'd lost an entire night's sleep because of the night sounds.

Yuki turned and saw that it was Papa. The hair over his bald spot was rumpled, and he squinted sleepily without his glasses.

"Well, Yuki," he said with a slow smile. "Since when do you eat your lunch at three o'clock in the morning?"

Yuki swallowed and grinned sheepishly. "I had the most horrible nightmare," she explained.

"Were you back in Topaz?"

Yuki nodded. "In the most awful dust storm! I was lost, and I couldn't breathe, and I thought I'd never see you or Mama again."

She shuddered as the despair of her nightmare overwhelmed her once more.

Papa sat down at the table beside her and patted her hand.

"It's strange," he said slowly. "I just had a vivid dream too."

"About Topaz?"

Papa poured himself some milk and buttered a piece of bread. "No, mine was a pleasant dream. We were home in Berkeley and we were in the backyard by the peach tree, you and I, trying to give Pepper a bath with the hose. Remember how he'd shake himself and spray everything within fifty feet with all that soap and water?"

Papa smiled as though he were seeing it all happening in front of him now.

Yuki grinned too, remembering. "And I'd get soap and water in my eyes and mouth and get soaking wet and . . ."

Suddenly a sharp deep longing to go back home to Berkeley flooded over her. "Papa, when can we go back?"

"I hope when the war is over, Yuki. When the United States and Japan stop fighting each other. When the hate is gone. Then maybe . . ."

"Only maybe?"

Papa rubbed his eyes and sighed. "Well, the Japanese are still excluded from the West Coast by law, and there are some people in California who don't want us ever to go back. They would have us kept out of the state forever."

"Forever?"

Was Papa saying they might never get to go home again? What would happen then to the thousands of Japanese who'd been uprooted from their homes and businesses and farms along the West Coast and were still in the concentration camps? Where would they all go if they couldn't go home to California after the war?

And what about us, Yuki wondered. Suppose they could never go back home. She couldn't bear even to think of such a thing. She thrust out her chin and said defiantly, "Well, I'm going back to California because that's where I was born, and that's where I belong, and nobody's going to keep me out!"

Papa gave her a look that held both surprise and pleasure.

"Good for you, Yuki," he said. "You hold onto that good thought, and maybe one day it will all come about."

2

YUKI HATED COMING HOME FROM SCHOOL ON TUESDAYS. That was one of the days Mama went to help Mrs. Griswold clean her house, and she wouldn't be home when Yuki got there. The apartment would be silent and empty, and Yuki would have to let herself in and sit in the lonely emptiness until Mama got home.

At least let there be some good mail today, she thought, and all the way home she sent messages to the mailbox to be stuffed with nice fat letters for her.

When she got home, she found their landlady, Mrs. Henley, sitting on the front porch with her husband. They were sitting in their rockers, each holding a Siamese cat, and watching the world go by.

"Afternoon, Yuki," Mrs. Henley called out.

"Hi, Mrs. Henley, Mr. Henley."

The old man was bundled up in a plaid blanket, looking like a race horse who'd just won a race. Mrs. Henley was keeping the autumn chill off his bones, she explained.

Yuki knew Mrs. Henley wanted to chat, but she could already see something in the mailbox and she longed to find out what it was. Besides, she wasn't crazy about chatting with Mrs. Henley, even though she did look the tiniest bit like her old friend, Mrs. Jamieson, who lived across the street from them in Berkeley. It was probably her pale crepey skin and the gray-green eyes. But of course her eyes didn't have the friendly warmth of Mrs. Jamieson's, and she didn't have the bright halo of flaming hair that Mrs. Jamieson dyed each month in remembrance of her late husband, Captain Jamieson, who had told her never ever to change. Mrs. Henley couldn't come close to being like Mrs. Jamieson, not in a million years.

Yuki thought longingly of the cozy warmth of Mrs. Jamieson's house with its scent of rose petals and spices, and of the hot cocoa they'd sip together as they looked at her collections of stamps and seashells and jewels. The day before Yuki and her family got sent to camp, Mrs. Jamieson had taken a beautiful gold and pearl ring from her jewelry box and given it to Yuki.

"Keep this for good luck, Yuki, dear," she'd told her, "and I know one day you'll come back home again."

But Yuki was afraid to take the ring into camp with her for fear she might lose it. Mama was storing all her valuables in a trunk at Bekins Van and Storage, so Yuki

put her ring in its black velvet box, then inside a pair of socks, and put it in Mama's trunk too.

There were a lot of things besides her valuables in Mama's trunk. There were things like packets of faded letters from her family in Japan, old diaries and photograph albums, and the drawings and clay animals that Ken and Yuki had made in grammar school. Mama saved everything. She couldn't bear to throw out anything that was special to her. So when the President of the United States ordered all the Japanese out of the West Coast, and the army gave them ten days to leave Berkeley, Mama didn't know where or how to begin.

"How can I pack our whole life into boxes and cartons in just ten days?" she asked desperately. "If only Papa were here."

But Papa was in a prisoner of war camp in Montana where he and hundreds of other Japanese businessmen and community leaders had been sent by the FBI the day the war broke out. All he could do was write letters that arrived full of holes cut out by the censors.

Mama grew more and more frantic as she counted the days until they had to leave. She put a "Furniture for Sale" sign in the front window and sold her nice sofa and dining room set to the first woman who inquired. She sold and gave away things she should have stored and stored things she should have thrown out.

She was so careful to obey every new order issued by the government that she even insisted Ken take his binoculars and camera to the police station when the Japanese were told to turn in all "contraband."

Ken was among the first to go and register as "head of household," and when he came home he had a handful of numbered baggage tags that were to be attached to everything they were permitted to take into camp.

"Look," he said dismally. "We're Family 13453 now."

Yuki tried out the sound of it and hated it. "Yuki Sakane, Number 13453." It made her feel like a prisoner.

Some nights, Yuki's best friend in Berkeley, Mimi Nelson, came from next door to see her, since Yuki could no longer go out after the eight o'clock curfew set for all Japanese.

"It's so stupid!" Mimi said indignantly. "What do they think you'd do after eight o'clock anyway?"

"Maybe go out and shoot somebody," Yuki answered dourly.

But Ken added quickly, "It's a lot more likely somebody'd take a shot at us!"

He was right. There were plenty of people in California who hated anybody with a Japanese face, and many of them carried guns. In fact, the parents of one of his college classmates had been shot and killed by vigilantes in one of the small valley towns.

On their last day in Berkeley, it was Mimi Nelson's mother who drove them to the civil control station where the Japanese of Berkeley were to report to be taken to camp. As they were leaving, Mrs. Jamieson hurried from across the street to say good-bye. She pinned a pink carnation from her garden on Mama's coat, saying, "I hope you'll be coming home soon, my dear."

Then she turned to Yuki and gave her a long, wordless hug. The last thing Yuki said to her was, "I stored your ring in Mama's trunk, Mrs. Jamieson. I'm saving it to wear when we all come home again."

And somehow that promise and the thought of the tiny gold ring waiting in its velvet box in the darkness of the trunk gave Yuki the hope that they really would go home again one day.

Yuki could never begin to love Mrs. Henley the way she loved Mrs. Jamieson, even though on the day they moved in, she had brought them a hot tuna noodle casserole.

She had the feeling that Mrs. Henley never quite trusted them. Once she'd asked Yuki why they had been sent to the concentration camp in the first place.

"Why would the President make all the Japanese leave the West Coast if you weren't dangerous?" she asked.

"Papa says there were a lot of reasons," Yuki explained. "It was partly panic and partly because there've always been people in California who wanted to get rid of us."

Mrs. Henley pursed her lips. "Well, it's possible you people might have tried to help Japan. After all, it *is* your country."

"But it's *not* my country. The United States is," Yuki said impatiently.

"But why would your own country put you behind barbed wire?"

"They never should have."

15

"Weren't there some Japanese who sent signals from their fishing boats?"

"No! Those were lies."

How could Mrs. Henley believe those stupid rumors? Yuki wished Ken were there to help explain everything to her. He'd know how. She tried hard to think what Ken might say.

"My brother Ken volunteered for the army from camp," she said, her voice rising, "even if his country put him in a concentration camp."

Mrs. Henley's eyebrows arched up in surprise. "He did?"

"Sure. So did his friend, Jim Hirai. They both went."

Yuki had never felt good about Mrs. Henley after that conversation. It had left her feeling bruised and let down. Mrs. Henley had not only disappointed her, she'd left Yuki feeling somehow ashamed of being Japanese. And Yuki hated that.

Yuki didn't want to talk to Mrs. Henley now or answer any more of her silly questions. She marched straight toward their mailbox and found two letters inside. She told Mrs. Henley she had homework to do, and she rushed upstairs to their apartment two steps at a time. She didn't even look at the letters until she was alone upstairs. She felt like Pepper taking his bone behind his house, waiting until no one was around to enjoy it. Some things needed to be savored in private without curious eyes watching.

Once she was upstairs, Yuki took the letters to the window seat where the afternoon sun filtered through

16

the gold-leafed maple, making lacy patterns that danced over the cushions.

The first letter was for Mama and Papa from their old friend, Mr. Toda, who seemed almost like a grandfather to her. He'd gone with them on their Sunday picnics and eaten holiday dinners with them and come often just to talk to Mama and Papa over a cup of tea. Whenever he came, he never forgot to bring something for Yuki. Sometimes it was a crisp white bag filled with jelly beans or fruit drops oozing with pink juices. Sometimes it was just a package of gum. He didn't quite know how to talk to her, so instead he had brought her the small child gifts that always pleased her. Now he was still in Topaz, living in the camp's bachelor quarters because he had no family of his own. Yuki gave his letter a little pat and, setting it aside, eagerly opened the second one, a bulging pink envelope addressed to her from Emi.

"Dear lucky Yuki on the outside," Emi began. "Do you know what Grandma said last night? She said we were staying right here in Topaz until we're allowed back in California. She said she couldn't leave Grandpa buried all alone out in the desert, and she's not leaving until we can dig up his bones and take him back to bury him in California where he belongs."

Yuki shuddered as she remembered how Emi's grandpa had been shot by a sentry in the guard tower who thought he was trying to escape. "He was only looking for arrowheads," she murmured now, saying again the words Grandma Kurihara had cried over and over when she heard what happened.

Yuki knew Emi's grandma was strong and determined. If she had made up her mind, she'd probably never change it. Poor Emi, Yuki thought, she'd never be able to come out to Salt Lake City now.

"Know what else Grandma said?" Emi's letter went on. "She said it's too dangerous to go outside. She said the Japanese are getting beat up and shot at because a lot of people still hate us. Do they? Are you scared?"

It wasn't that Yuki was scared. It was just that she didn't feel comfortable. No matter where she went, she felt that people saw her as the enemy just because she looked Japanese. But Salt Lake City was a lot better than California. She wished she could make Grandma Kurihara understand. Even if you were scared, it was better to be free than to be kept inside a barbed wire fence. She knew Papa could find her a job if only she'd come out here.

But it had been many weeks before Papa himself had found a job. He said nobody wanted to hire an enemy alien just out of camp and one who was also paroled from a prisoner of war camp before that.

"But you didn't do anything wrong," Yuki defended Papa. "Tell them the FBI sent you to that POW camp just because you worked for a Japanese company in San Francisco. That's all."

Papa had looked bleak. "Well, that's reason enough for some people not to want me. Besides," he added, "no one seems to need an ex-manager of a Japanese shipping company."

That was why Mama had gotten a job first through

their landlady. She went to work for a rich white lady with eight children.

"Eight children!" Yuki gasped when Mama first told her.

No wonder they needed Mama to help them clean house. In fact, Mrs. Griswold had asked her to come every day to wash for them as well, but Papa wouldn't allow it. Mama had trouble with her back and Papa worried about her.

"It's bad enough you have to work at all, Mama," he said soberly. "I'm certainly not going to have you doing another family's wash."

"I'd be willing, Papa, until you find work."

But Papa wouldn't hear of it. "Your father would climb out of his grave and haunt me if I allowed you to wash the soiled garments of someone else's family."

Mama smiled faintly at the thought. "He might at that," she murmured, "even though many Japanese women have had to do it."

Yuki's grandfathers had died in Japan long before she was born. They had both been brave samurai warriors in years long past, and that was something to be proud of. It meant Yuki and her brother were the grandchildren of two samurai, so they had to be brave and courageous and loyal too. It meant being strong when necessary, but still having a gentle heart capable of loving beautiful things. It meant they had a past to live up to, and Yuki wasn't sure she could manage.

For her, Japan was an alien land she'd never seen, and her grandfathers seemed more like people she'd read about than anybody linked to her by blood. If she died and met up with them in Heaven, she might not even recognize them. She imagined them to be rather fierce-looking gentlemen, splendid in samurai armor, wearing swords at their sides and carrying bannered spears.

They'd probably take one look at her and sniff. "Who is this strange, ignorant creature who has black hair and brown eyes like ours, but speaks only the language of the foreigner?"

And Yuki would have to look down at her toes and say, "I'm Yuki Sakane, your twelve-year-old grandchild, but I didn't go to Japanese language school to study Japanese like Mama wanted me to."

Sometimes Yuki looked at herself and thought it strange that she looked so Japanese when she didn't feel very Japanese inside. Her black hair had no trace of a wave or curl. Her brown eyes were not as wide as Emi's nor double-lidded as Mama's were. She was just an ordinary, round-faced Nisei born in California but neither totally American nor totally Japanese.

Eventually Papa found a job as a shipping clerk in a department store downtown. He had been pushed back to doing the kind of work he might have done when he first arrived from Japan. It was as though he'd suddenly lost almost thirty years of his life and work.

But Papa only said, "*Shikata ga nai.* It can't be helped. Some people have lost everything, and young men are losing their lives in this war. At least I'm alive and healthy and that's something to be thankful for."

Mama felt bad that Papa had to be a shipping clerk when he had the brains and experience to be the manager of the store. And Papa felt bad that Mama had to be somebody's cleaning woman when she should have been at home growing flowers and writing poetry and not straining her back. But that's the way things were and there was no changing them.

Yuki hurried through the rest of Emi's seven-page letter and came to the last paragraph.

"Try hard to think of a way we can get Grandma to go out to Salt Lake City," she wrote. "And please answer immediately. I WANT TO GET OUT!!! Desperately yours, Emi."

3

"YUKI, I'M HOME." IT WAS MAMA.

"We got some mail," Yuki shouted as soon as she heard her mother coming up the stairs.

"From your brother?"

"No, but two letters from Topaz. Mama, how can we make Emi's grandma come out of camp?"

Mama sighed, trying to hide her disappointment at not hearing from Ken.

"Yuki, we can't make her do anything she doesn't want to do." Mama understood how Grandma Kurihara felt about leaving her husband behind buried all alone in the desert. "You've got to wait until she's ready," she said softly.

"Oh gloom," Yuki muttered. "She won't be ready until the war ends and that might not be for another ten years."

Mama wasn't listening. She had put on her glasses

and was reading Mr. Toda's letter, the wrinkles gathering around her eyes in a slow, easy smile.

"Mr. Toda sent me one of his poems," she explained.

Old Mr. Toda had never written a poem in his entire life, until he was sent to camp. Then it was as though all his lonely longing came tumbling out, caught now in the delicate web of poetry.

"Read it to me," Yuki said.

But when Mama began to read aloud, it was as though Yuki were listening to a bagful of sounds that made no sense. She couldn't understand the poetic Japanese words.

It was the same when Yuki listened to the poems Mama scribbled on a scrap of paper or the edge of a newspaper. Mama tried to explain them to her, but it was like trying to describe the smell of a rose. The poems were Mama's secret other self, a shadowy presence, and Yuki could only guess at understanding the things Mama felt deep inside and couldn't tell anyone, not even Papa.

What Papa wrote were things like business letters and checks. He also kept a ledger of their household accounts with neat columns of figures that had their own special meaning for him. He took care of all the bills because he said if he left that to Mama, she'd probably write poetry on the back of the bills and forget all about paying them.

But Yuki knew Papa was proud of Mama's poems. He told her to send them to the Japanese newspaper and try to get them published.

"Well, maybe . . . someday," was all Mama would

say, however, and she never even copied her poems on a clean sheet of paper. It was as though she felt that for now she should keep her poetry on the outer fringes of her life.

Yuki waited for Mama to tell her what Mr. Toda had written, but all she said was, "I wish we had room here for Mr. Toda and could get him out of camp." She was silent for a few minutes and then said, "Well, someday Mr. Toda will be free, and so will Emi and her grandma. We just have to be patient."

"I wish this darn war would hurry up and end so we can all go back to California," Yuki said wistfully. "Then everything will be perfect again."

Mama looked thoughtful. "I hope so, Yuki," she said. "I surely hope so."

She stood up then and put on her apron. "I'm making one of Papa's favorites tonight—fried noodles with pork."

"How come? Is it a special day?"

"No, I just thought he might need some cheering up today," Mama answered vaguely and disappeared into the kitchen.

Yuki didn't have time to wonder why. If she hurried, she'd just have time to write Emi a quick note before Papa came home.

Nov. 3, 1944

Miss Emi Kurihara
Block 7, Barrack 5, Room 2-a
Topaz, Utah
Dearest Emi:

Here I am answering your letter immediately, just like you told me to. I think your grandma's crazy to

24

want to stay in camp, but Mama says we can't make her come out if she doesn't want to. Besides, I guess she wouldn't want to be anybody's cleaning lady out here in Salt Lake City anyway.

Yuki grinned at the mere thought of anybody telling Grandma Kurihara what to do. If anybody was giving orders, it would have to be Emi's grandma. She liked being in charge of things, the way she was when she had her own grocery store in San Francisco. It wasn't that she was always bossy and stubborn. There was probably a gathering of gentle thoughts somewhere inside the old woman, Yuki thought, but she wasn't like Mama. She could seldom show them to anyone. Not even to Emi.

"Well, never mind," Yuki continued. "One of these days . . ."

She had to stop, for she heard Papa coming in downstairs.

"*Tadaima*, I'm home," he called.

The wonderful smell of fried pork and onions was drifting through their apartment and down the steps to welcome him, but instead of remarking how good supper smelled, Papa slumped wearily into his big armchair.

"Wretched creature," he muttered.

"Who—me, Papa?"

"No, no, Yuki. Of course not you."

Mama came from the kitchen still holding her long cooking chopsticks. "How did it go today, Papa?" she asked.

"More of the same," Papa answered with a long sigh.

Then Yuki remembered. It was the day of the month Papa had to report to the parole officer at the Immigration Board. She still felt a stab of anger when she recalled how the three FBI men had taken Papa away like a common criminal. But he had been one of the lucky ones, released early to join them in Topaz. Now that he was out of camp, however, he had to report to a parole officer each month and would have to until the war ended.

"What'd he want to know today?" Yuki asked.

"He asked in which direction I would shoot if I had a gun and was standing between American and Japanese soldiers."

"*Mah!*" Mama was flabbergasted.

"So what'd you say, Papa?"

Papa took off his glasses and rubbed his eyes. The question was so ridiculous, he began now to smile at the thought of it.

"What could I say?" he asked with a shrug. "I told him I'd point the gun straight up and shoot at the sun."

"And then what'd he say?"

"He made me fill out the same fifteen-page questionnaire all over again."

No wonder Papa was in a bad mood. But his black moods never lasted long, and already his anger was melting away. "I suppose the poor fool only thought he was doing his job."

"Well, it's over until next month," Mama comforted. "Now come and enjoy your fried noodles. You'll feel better."

Papa got up and started toward the kitchen. But before he left the living room, Yuki saw him take the evening newspaper from his coat pocket and stuff it quickly into the wastepaper basket. That was strange because Papa never threw out a paper until it was at least a day old. Was there something in the paper that Papa didn't want them to see? Yuki intended to find out as soon as supper was over.

AS SOON AS SHE COULD, YUKI RETRIEVED PAPA'S NEWS-
paper from the wastepaper basket and took it to her
room. She found the article about the 442nd RCT and
now she knew why Papa had hidden it from Mama.

The 442 had been sent to France and was in a
terrible, bloody battle in the forests of the Vosges
Mountains trying to rescue a battalion cut off from
water, food, and medical supplies. The words "wither-
ing enemy fire" kept echoing in her mind as Yuki read
about the steep, rugged mountain forest dotted with
mines, and the artillery shells exploding against the
trees and showering the men with shrapnel.

Yuki felt weak in the knees just thinking of Ken
in the midst of all that terror. And when she went to
sleep that night, her nightmares shifted from the dust
storms of Topaz to the battle in the Vosges Mountains.

It was raining and cold, and somehow Yuki was over there with Ken, struggling up a slippery mountain path, with a full pack on her back and an M-1 rifle in her hand. She could hear the German shells coming closer and closer as she slogged through miles of mud, watching closely not to step on a mine. Her bones ached, her eyes burned from lack of sleep, and she could feel the cold rain seeping through her clothes, wet and damp against her skin.

She was trying hard to catch up with Ken, but he was "going for broke," giving everything he had, trying to prove he was a good American. And he wouldn't wait for her.

"Ken!" she shouted, but he never turned around, and soon he disappeared entirely into the mountain mists.

"Ken!" she called out a second desperate time. Then she woke up shivering.

What did soldiers do when it rained, Yuki wondered. How did they ever get their socks dry? Suppose all Ken had was a cold, muddy foxhole to jump into, with water puddling up all around, his boots and socks soaked through? Suppose Ken got killed before he could ever have a nice hot meal or sleep again in a warm, dry bed? Yuki couldn't bear even to think about it.

"Kenichi Sakane," she murmured. "You'd just better not get yourself killed over there, or I'll never ever forgive you."

The next evening Yuki broke Mama's best crystal bud vase. Mama had wrapped it up in her gray wool sweater and carried it with her all the way from Berkeley to Topaz in the desert, and finally to Salt Lake City. It was a special vase she used when she put a flower beside the photographs of Yuki's grandparents on the anniversary day of their death. It was the vase she used too for Hana, the older sister Yuki had never seen, who had died when she was only one year old and was buried in the cemetery in the hills of Oakland.

Mama never talked about Hana, but she always kept a snapshot of her on the bureau. It was turning brown now, but the silver frame it was in was always polished and shiny. It would have been nice, Yuki sometimes thought, to have a sister who'd always be there to do things with.

The day before they had to leave Berkeley and go to the concentration camp, Mama had gone to the cemetery to say good-bye to Hana. She took her a bouquet of all the flowers she could gather from their garden and told her not to worry. She told her Papa was in a prisoner of war camp and the rest of them were about to be sent to another kind of camp, but they'd all be back when the war was over, and for her to rest in peace until then. She had pulled out the weeds around the small gray tombstone and then watered one last time the flowering cherry tree she and Papa had planted there.

And now Yuki had broken Mama's crystal vase and she'd never have it again to put beside Hana's picture, or anybody else's. It had slipped through her soapy fingers just as she was putting it on the dish rack and crashed to the floor in a mass of sharp, jagged pieces.

Yuki felt so awful she wanted to cry. She usually didn't cry when she'd done something stupid. Sometimes she just tried to cover it up by acting as though it weren't important. Another time she might have swept up the pieces before Mama saw them and used her own money to buy her another bud vase.

But tonight it was different. She knew how much the vase meant to Mama, and she also had this terrible feeling that it was a bad omen. It meant something had happened to Ken. She just knew it. All day she'd had these anxious feelings about Ken and now she knew why. Something had happened to him, and maybe she'd never see him again.

"Oh Mama," Yuki wailed.

Mama put her arms around her and held her close. "That's all right, Yuki," she said. "It was an accident."

And then as though she knew exactly what Yuki was thinking, she said, "Look at it this way, Yuki. Maybe my vase was broken in order to spare your brother. Maybe it was destroyed in place of something happening to Ken."

Mama smiled a sort of half-smile, as though she were remembering something from long ago. "That's what your grandma would have said, Yuki. She used to say that objects sometimes have lives of their own and that sometimes they die in order to spare us."

Yuki knew Mama was trying to make her feel better. Mama swept up the broken pieces of glass and put them in a newspaper. She folded the newspaper neatly and carefully, almost as though it were a gift. Then she laid it gently in the garbage can, giving the

vase a sort of burial rather than just dumping it out unceremoniously.

"There," she said, brushing her hands. "Now I think I'll write a letter to your brother."

Mama had already written him two letters that week, but they hadn't had a letter from Ken in over a month.

"No news is good news," Papa said.

But suppose Ken were wounded, Yuki thought, and his company had moved on without him. Suppose nobody found him and he was lying there in the rain, bleeding to death and . . .

Yuki felt a sharp sadness that surfaced into a sob.

She found one more piece of glass that Mama had missed and dropped it carefully into the trash can. She almost felt as though she'd killed Ken herself.

CHAPTER

5

CHRISTMAS HAD SEEMED SAD AND EMPTY THIS YEAR BE-
cause for the first time in her life Yuki didn't have any
close friends to share it with.

Mama did her best to bring the Christmas spirit
into their apartment. She bought a small crèche at the
five and ten cents store and put it up on the table in
the living room.

Mary and Joseph and the baby Jesus were there,
surrounded by the animals of the barnyard and the
shepherds and the three wisemen with their gifts. It
was beautiful and peaceful, as though Bethlehem were
right there in their living room.

"Maybe the world has gone crazy," Mama said,
"but the Christmas story is still the same. It's important
to remember that, Yuki, and not forget what Christmas
really means."

"Uh-huh."

Yuki understood. But she couldn't help wishing things were different.

"Don't keep wishing for what can't be," Papa told her. "Be happy for this special Christmas we have now."

But Yuki thought of the Christmases back home in Berkeley when the house was filled with the tantalizing smell of Mama's cookies baking in the oven and the glorious fresh green smell of the Christmas tree by the front window. This year Mama was too busy to do all the things she used to do back home.

Yuki remembered the Christmas Eves when she delivered Mama's cookies to the neighbors, and Mrs. Jamieson would ask her to stay for a cup of sweet, creamy cocoa.

Then there was the Christmas program at their small Japanese church, all decorated with red and green paper streamers and bells, and a giant Christmas tree with enormous colored balls and silver tinsel. The church was always crowded on Christmas Eve when the Sunday School put on its program.

Yuki remembered how cold it was in the drafty parsonage parlor where they changed into their costumes for the nativity scene, squealing and shivering around the small gas heater as they shook off their heavy coats and new Christmas clothes. Yuki was usually one of the angels, dressed in scratchy white gauze with a silver halo that slithered down on her forehead. She giggled and whispered with her friends until it was time to appear on stage. But once she was in her place and the choir sang "O Holy Night," somehow the special feeling of Christmas wrapped her up like a comforting blanket on a cold, foggy night.

Afterwards, Mama and Papa's friends gathered around, telling her in their soft Japanese voices how beautiful the program had been. Maybe that was part of it, Yuki thought now. She missed her own friends, but she missed Mama and Papa's friends too, with their Japanese talk and their genial bows and even the smelly yellow pickles they brought to picnics. Maybe that's what was wrong with this Christmas. Here in Salt Lake City their world was made up only of *hakujin*—white people who were strangers to them in a strange city that wasn't home.

The doorbell suddenly jangled Yuki out of her dreams. Papa was at work and Mama had ventured out, though it was snowing hard, bundled up in her warmest coat and scarf, to buy groceries. "We have to eat," she'd said, "snowstorm or not."

Yuki ran down the steps, saw a shadowy person on the other side of the lace-covered glass of the front door, and wondered who it could be. When she opened the door, she saw it was a boy with a telegram, and she wanted to slam the door shut and pretend he had never come. She had an awful feeling he'd brought terrible news about Ken. She'd known something had happened to him from the moment she'd broken Mama's crystal bud vase.

Mrs. Henley was just coming up the front steps, trudging heavily in her boots and her shabby fur coat with its frayed cuffs where the leather was beginning to show. She saw what Yuki held in her hand.

"It's not bad news is it, Yuki?" she asked.

"I . . . I don't know."

"Is your mama home?"

Yuki shook her head. "She's gone to the market."

Mrs. Henley's face was red from the wind and her breath came in short gasps that left wisps of steam in the brittle, cold air.

Yuki was surprised by the gentleness in her voice. "Don't fret now, my dear," she said softly. "Do you want me to open it for you?"

Yuki nodded. Her throat was tight and dry, and her heart felt as though it might explode. She couldn't talk and she could scarcely think. She was glad to hand the envelope to Mrs. Henley, as though by giving it to her she could be rid of the awful news inside.

Mrs. Henley pulled off her damp gloves and ripped open the envelope. And then she smiled. "Why, Yuki, it's all right," she said brightly. "Your brother's only been wounded. He's been evacuated to a hospital, but he's all right. Maybe he'll even be sent home soon."

Then for the first time she gave Yuki a warm, loving hug, and Yuki hugged her back.

It was funny how the telegram about Ken made them all so happy. Here poor Ken was lying in some hospital with shrapnel wounds in his leg, but Mama and Papa and Yuki were overjoyed because Ken hadn't been killed.

"It's all right now, Mama," Papa said over and over again. "Ken is alive."

And Mama couldn't stop crying because she was

so relieved. None of them had dared speak aloud what each feared, but Yuki knew she wasn't the only one who had feared the worst.

"Mrs. Henley said maybe he'd get sent home soon," Yuki said hopefully.

"Oh I do hope so," Mama answered. "I can't believe he's really all right until I see him with my own eyes." Then she said something else.

"You know, good things often happen in threes. Maybe two more nice things will happen before long."

As usual, Mama was right. A few weeks later, Papa heard that the army had revoked the exclusion order against the Japanese on the West Coast.

Yuki had never seen him so excited in a long time.

"Do you know what that means?" he asked, pacing back and forth in the living room because he couldn't sit still.

"It means we can go back to California now if we want to. It means we can go home to Berkeley. The army can't keep us out any more."

Yuki leaped from her chair and hung on Papa's neck as she used to do when she was little.

"Can we go home then, Papa? Can we go back to Berkeley?"

"I don't see why not," Papa answered quickly. "I'm sure I can find a sponsor there to vouch for me."

"But where will we live?" Mama wondered. "Our old house is rented now to someone else."

"We'll find something," Papa assured her. "Don't worry. We'll find a way." And he went straight to the desk and began writing some letters.

It was a while before the third good thing happened, but it finally did. The Reverend Wada wrote to Papa that he'd gotten permission to leave Camp Topaz and was going back to their Japanese church in Berkeley.

"My wife and I will open our church again and turn it into a hostel so the returning Japanese will have a place to stay until they can find proper housing," he wrote. "Won't you and your family join us as soon as possible and help us open up our church once more? I will secure a sponsor for you, Mr. Sakane, and do whatever is necessary to facilitate your return."

Now they had a place to go and California could no longer keep them out.

"Start packing, Mama," Papa said as soon as he read the Reverend Wada's letter. "We're going home."

6

YUKI HAD NEVER THOUGHT SHE'D FEEL SAD ABOUT LEAV-ing Salt Lake City and saying good-bye to Mr. and Mrs. Henley, but she did, just a little. Each time she had to say good-bye to someone, it was as though she were leaving behind a small piece of herself. She'd already had so many partings since the war began, from her friends in Berkeley, then from Ken, and last year from her friends in Topaz. If she had to say many more farewells, she felt as though there'd soon be nothing left of her old self.

When Yuki said so to Mama, she got one of those thoughtful looks that came over her face when she had an idea for a poem.

"That's all right, Yuki," she said. "It's nice to leave a bit of ourselves with our friends, isn't it? Then we go on to new things and new places, and maybe we become different and more interesting people."

Yuki hadn't thought of it like that. Maybe she was already so different Mrs. Jamieson or Mimi Nelson wouldn't even know her when she got back to Berkeley. She'd grown two inches and gained six pounds from all the beans and potatoes and bread she'd eaten in camp. And she knew her face looked different. The desert sun and wind had tanned it to the color of dark toast, and the long months in the desert had left her with a bleak, lonely look.

On the morning they were to leave Salt Lake City, Mrs. Henley came upstairs with a box of sandwiches and fruit and cookies for them to eat on the train.

"Come back and visit us someday when the war is over," she said to Yuki.

"Okay, Mrs. Henley," Yuki said. But deep in her heart she knew she didn't mean it. She didn't ever want to come back to Utah again. For her Utah would always mean Topaz, the concentration camp in the desert. It would mean the choking dust storms and the place where Emi's grandfather was shot to death, leaving Emi with no one else in the world except her grandma. But she gave Mrs. Henley a small hug and thanked her for the lunch to eat on the train.

A cold shiver of nervous excitement surged through her as Yuki waited with Mama and Papa for their train to glide into the crowded station. She felt jumpy and a little scared, like the time they were released from camp and came outside. Yuki carried a bulging shopping bag stuffed with the last-minute things she couldn't squeeze into her suitcase, and she tried hard to be small and quiet and inconspicuous so no one would notice her or hate her for being Japanese. When the train came in, it was crowded with soldiers on leave and with women and children going to see their husbands and fathers in military camps. Yuki knew some of the soldiers were on their way to the Pacific to join the battle against Japan.

She stayed close to Mama and Papa, following them quickly to their seats in the crowded coach. She was relieved to see that the chairs were soft and comfortable and not like the stiff, hard seats they'd sat on for three days when they rode the train out to Utah.

"Look, Mama, the seats lean back," Yuki said, testing her own chair. But Mama quickly warned her to push her chair back up. "You mustn't bother the people behind us," she said firmly. "You mustn't make a nuisance of yourself."

They had to be careful not to annoy anybody. But even if Yuki did nothing, there were some people who became angry anyway. It happened the first night when Yuki went to the restroom at the rear of their coach. Just as she opened the door to go in, a blond woman with two small children pushed past her. She glared angrily at Yuki and muttered, "Go back where you belong, you damn Jap."

She said it in such a low voice, at first Yuki couldn't believe she'd actually heard the words. But when she saw the look of hate on the woman's face, she knew the woman had not only said it, she'd really meant it.

Yuki felt as though she'd been kicked in the

stomach. She felt so awful she couldn't even tell Mama about it when she went back to her seat. It seemed somehow shameful to repeat the horrible words, as though by saying them again she would spread more filth on herself and on Mama as well.

After that, Yuki never went back to use the restroom in their coach. Instead, she walked two cars forward to use another one and often she asked Mama to go with her. Mama never asked her why, she just went with her. Maybe Mama knew without Yuki's telling her what had happened. Maybe the blond woman had spat her hateful words at Mama too.

As the train made its way westward through wide plains and deserts and small, sleepy towns, Yuki felt as though it would never get to California.

"I can't stand being on this train another minute," she complained to Mama.

But Mama reminded her how much nicer this was than the long train ride going in the other direction. Of course she was right. On the train to Topaz, there had been car captains assigned to each coach. They saw to it that the shades were kept drawn from sunset to sunrise and that no one left his car to go to another except twice a day at specified times. They had been allowed to get off the train only once during the three-day trip, and that was for ten minutes in the middle of a Nevada desert while armed soldiers stood guard so no one would try to escape.

This time they were free to do whatever they wished. Yuki got off and ran around at every station where the train stopped, rushing to the small stands to buy magazines and orange pop and candy bars and peanuts.

The last morning was the longest of all. "Papa, are we almost there?"

"The conductor said we were two hours late, Yuki. It'll probably be close to three o'clock by the time we get to Berkeley."

Three o'clock! Yuki had been awake since six that morning, partly because all her bones ached from sitting for so long, but mostly because she was so excited at the thought of finally reaching California.

"Who do you think will be there to meet us, Mama?"

"Why Reverend Wada, I expect."

"Anybody else?"

Mama knew Yuki had written to Mrs. Jamieson and Mimi telling them of their arrival on the "City of San Francisco."

"Don't count on anybody else," Mama cautioned. "You know Mrs. Jamieson is lame, and with Mimi's mama working at the defense plant now, you mustn't expect Mimi either."

"Uh-huh."

Yuki knew all that as well as Mama. Still, she couldn't help hoping somebody besides the Reverend Wada would be there so it would seem like a real homecoming.

It was impossible for Yuki to sit still until three o'clock. She couldn't concentrate on any of the books in her shopping bag. She got tired of looking out the window. She chewed two packages of Juicy Fruit gum and ate three small bags of salted peanuts. Then she had to climb over Mama so many times to go for a drink of water that Mama finally made her sit in the aisle seat. After a while, Yuki changed places with Papa, so he could sit with Mama and she sat in the aisle seat across from them.

At last, when she thought she couldn't bear another minute on the train, Yuki saw the smoky old brick buildings of Crockett, close to the waters of Carquinez Strait, and she knew they were almost there. It wouldn't be long now. She watched eagerly for the first glimpse of San Francisco Bay and then for the buildings of Berkeley edged up to the water and spreading back into the hills to the east.

At last the conductor called out, "Next stop, Berkeley. This way out." The train began to slow down, slipping past wigwagging signs blinking and clanging to hold back the cars. Then Yuki saw the round cream-colored dome of the depot with its "Berkeley" sign, and she could no longer contain herself.

"Mama! Papa! We're here!" she shouted. And without waiting for them, she ran ahead and was the first person to get off the train.

Almost immediately she saw the Reverend Wada, dressed up in his best black suit, waving a shabby felt hat. Yuki waved back, and then turned to urge Mama and Papa to hurry. When she looked again, she saw the green coat and the fluff of red hair under an enormous green hat.

"Mrs. Jamieson!" Yuki shouted, running toward her. "You came! You came!"

Mrs. Jamieson wrapped her up in a warm hug that smelled of lavender and cloves. "You didn't think I'd let you come home and not find me here to greet you, did you? I've been reminding Reverend Wada every day for the past week to bring me along to the station."

Yuki looked around. "Did Mimi come?"

"She couldn't come, Yuki, but she sent her love. So did her mama and papa."

"Oh. Well, never mind."

"The important thing is that you're back at last," Mrs. Jamieson reminded her.

And of course she was right. That was all that really mattered, and coming home to Mrs. Jamieson was all the welcome Yuki needed, at least for now.

7

IT SEEMED STRANGE BEING BACK IN BERKELEY AND YET
not being able to go to their old house. They could
only look at it from across the street when they dropped
off Mrs. Jamieson.

"It just hasn't been the same since you left," she
murmured as she struggled out of the car. "I hardly
know the new family there."

Yuki looked at the neat stucco bungalow with the
wide front porch where she had often sat with Pepper
on a long summer's day. "Maybe someday those people
will move and then we can rent it again and everything'll be like it was," she said hopefully.

But no one was listening to her. Mama was peering out the car window trying to see how the garden
looked. "The camellias aren't blooming," she observed

quietly. "And neither is the wisteria. Shouldn't they be in bloom by now, Papa?"

Papa didn't seem to want to see what had become of their beautiful garden. "Nothing stays the same, Mama," he pointed out. "You'll only be disappointed if you think nothing ever changes."

Although he spoke to Mama, it was Yuki he was looking at. It was as though he wanted her to understand something he'd already learned himself.

But Papa's wrong, Yuki thought. Mrs. Jamieson hadn't changed at all. She was every bit as nice as she'd always been, and Yuki loved her just as much. Before she could say so, however, the Reverend Wada lifted his hat and started up the engine.

"See you soon, Mrs. Jamieson," Yuki called. And they were on their way to the Japanese church.

"I hope you aren't expecting too much," the Reverend Wada said a bit apologetically. "The old house behind the church that we always used for a student dormitory is in pretty bad shape. It needs a lot of cleaning before we can use it as a hostel."

"But there is a place for us to sleep tonight?" Papa asked cautiously.

"Oh yes, don't worry." The Reverend Wada waved a thin hand to brush aside Papa's concerns. "Everything is arranged. We've borrowed some cots and put them in the chapel and the parsonage and . . . well, you'll soon see."

Now the car pulled into the graveled driveway beside the church. Yuki thought it still looked almost the same, with its tall bell tower that had a cross, but never had had a bell. Yet it seemed shabbier and somehow battered, with gray streaks running down the sides of the building and paper patches on its cracked windows.

Mrs. Wada hurried from the parsonage to greet them, with her three small children swarming around her. They surrounded Yuki, pulling at her coat, wanting her to see where they were all going to sleep that night.

"Come look," they urged in high, excited voices. "We're going to sleep with the organ."

Yuki let herself be pulled inside the church and turned toward the dim, high-ceilinged chapel. The last of the afternoon sun filtered through the tall, arched windows, giving the dark wood paneling a warm, earthy glow. It seemed strange to see the chapel empty, without the usual clusters of people sitting in the pews, the dark-suited men on the left of the center aisle and the women, in their Sunday hats and coats, sitting on the right.

It felt odd not to see the Reverend Wada standing at the pulpit in his black morning coat, raising his voice so it reached out to the very last row. It always surprised Yuki that such a large voice could come from such a frail man.

The children clattered noisily down the center aisle to the back of the chapel, looking to see if Yuki were following. Then they raced up the steps to the small balcony that held the church organ.

"Look," they said, grinning with pleasure. "Here's where we sleep tonight."

In the far corner of the balcony, Yuki saw the old

reed organ with its faded green foot pedals. It was covered up with a wrinkled sheet, and in front of it were six army cots lined up as though they were in a tent at summer camp.

"Am I sleeping up here too?" Yuki asked.

The children nodded. "You're taking care of us."

"Oh. And where do my mama and papa sleep?"

"In our room in the parsonage."

Yuki swallowed the knot of disappointment that welled up inside her. This wasn't exactly what she'd expected.

"Well, you knew you were staying at the church, didn't you?" she asked herself. "You knew it was a hostel now. You knew you couldn't go back to the old house across from Mrs. Jamieson's."

Yes, she knew all that. Still, there was something lonely and sad about the musty, empty church that had been used by strangers while they were in camp. She'd expected to feel happier at being back.

As soon as the three Wada children calmed down and went to sleep that night, Yuki composed a letter to Emi in her head.

"It feels weird sleeping here in the empty church with the old organ covered up like a big white ghost and three kids sound asleep next to me," she began.

Then she decided the situation called for something more direct. "Hurry up and come back before somebody else takes the two empty cots next to mine," she said, sending one of her mental messages. "You too, Mr. Toda," she continued. "Hurry on back." And Ken. What should she say to Ken?

Before she had decided, she felt asleep, and the next thing she knew, something had leaped on her stomach and was walking slowly toward her neck.

"Eeeee! Help!" Yuki let out a terrible screech and wondered if she were having another nightmare. She sat bolt upright on her cot and discovered it was already morning. The sun was streaming into the balcony from the circular window behind her. The three Wada children were gone, their beds empty and unmade. And the horrible creature that had given her such a scare was only a striped alley cat.

Yuki didn't like cats. "Scat! Shoo! Get out!" She jumped on her cot and threw her pillow at the cat. With a startled yowl, it leaped away and scampered toward the organ where it disappeared beneath the sheet.

"Here now! That's no way to treat my cat!"

Yuki turned to see a short, heavy-set man with wild, bushy gray hair that looked a little like a bird's nest. His steel-rimmed spectacles were halfway down his nose, and he wore a pair of rumpled trousers and a shirt that needed mending. He gave her a disapproving look.

"Hokusai was only being friendly," he said dourly. "He's a fine cat, and he's named after a famous Japanese artist. But I suppose you wouldn't know about things like that."

Yuki slid quickly back under the covers and pulled them up to her nose. "I don't like cats," she said firmly. And then, so she wouldn't sound too mean, she added, "But I love dogs."

The old man made no comment. He was on his

hands and knees crawling around the dusty floor, trying to find his cat. "Come, Hokusai," he called. "*Sah, oide, oide.* Pay no attention to this cross young lady."

"I'm not a cross . . ." Yuki began.

But now the old man took a piece of dried fish from his pocket and held it out for the cat. "Come, Hokusai. Come."

Quickly the cat emerged from under the sheet, flicked its tail and rubbed gently against the old man's legs before it nibbled at the fish.

"There, you see," the old man said. "I told you he was a fine cat. Maybe he'll even get to like you someday."

Then he picked up his cat in the crook of his arm and, speaking softly to it in Japanese, he clattered noisily down the stairs.

Yuki didn't see the old man again until that night at supper, but she did see his cat roaming around the parsonage.

"I'm sorry about throwing that pillow at you," she said to it. "I guess you can't help it if you're a cat."

Hokusai looked at her for a long time, whiskers twitching, yellow eyes staring, and then stalked off with an imperial air, and Yuki didn't know if she'd been forgiven or not.

Mama helped Mrs. Wada cook a good supper of rice and stew that evening, with plenty of pickled cabbage to eat at the end of the meal. Yuki saw the old man take two helpings of everything, and then lean back in his chair to enjoy a cigarette.

Papa talked to him as though he were an old

friend. "Well, Mr. Oka," he said, "tell us what luck you had today. Were you able to make arrangements to buy back your grocery store?"

A frown quickly swept over the old man's face. "Miller won't sell my Sunshine Grocery back to me unless I pay him five thousand dollars cash and take over the lease." The old man took a quick puff of his cigarette and added, "Do you know what he paid me for the shop when I was forced to sell it to him and go to camp?"

"Probably not much," Papa guessed.

"All of four hundred dollars, for the stock on my shelves, all the fixtures, and the good will I'd built up in the neighborhood for ten years."

The old man scowled and drew in a noisy gulp of tea. He shook his head sadly. "Scoundrels," he muttered darkly. "They're all scoundrels."

Mama knew what Mr. Oka was thinking. "Not all, Mr. Oka. Not all," she said quickly and went to the kitchen to return with a two-layer chocolate cake dripping with thick frosting and sprinkled with nuts.

"Look what our friend, Mrs. Jamieson, sent over to us today. She said it was to welcome us all back. That includes you too, Mr. Oka."

"And on Saturday ten students from the campus church are coming to help us paint the old dormitory in back," the Reverend Wada added.

"Cake and paint are all fine and good," Mr. Oka admitted, "but what I need now is some cash to buy back my old Sunshine Grocery, and who's going to give me that? Who can give me back the business I lost?"

Papa looked thoughtful. "Maybe we can find a way to help you, Mr. Oka," he said slowly. "We're all going to have to work together to get back on our feet again."

Yuki wondered how Papa was ever going to help the old man when he had no job himself. The Japanese shipping company he worked for no longer existed and he needed to find a house for them to rent too. Papa certainly had a lot to do before he could help Mr. Oka.

"Papa," Yuki began, when she felt something nudge her foot. Then she felt a soft, furry body sweep past her legs. She looked down and let out such a scream that Mama dropped her teacup and spilled tea all over the table.

"It's a dead mouse!" Yuki shouted, at which point, everybody rose very quickly from the table. But Mr. Oka came to pick up the small gray mouse by the tail.

"Well, well," he said, looking pleased. "Hokusai has brought you one of his gifts. I guess he's forgiven you, in spite of the way you treated him this morning."

When he'd disposed of the mouse, he returned saying, "If Hokusai says you're a friend, then I guess I accept you as well." And thrusting a rough, calloused hand at Yuki, he shook her hand solemnly with a firm, hard grip.

Yuki wasn't sure why, but it seemed important to be considered his friend.

"Thanks, Mr. Oka," she said. "Thanks a lot."

8

"YOU CAN HAVE ONE OF THE SECOND FLOOR ROOMS IN the back dormitory if you're willing to clean it up," the Reverend Wada told Yuki the next morning.

"I'm willing! I'm willing!" Yuki answered eagerly.

She was longing to have a room of her own where she could put in two extra cots for Emi and her grandma. Papa had already guaranteed a home for them and Mr. Toda when they returned, and he'd also made sure Mrs. Kurihara could bring her husband's remains back with her.

Cleaning up the old dormitory was much more work than Yuki thought it would be. Even Papa and the Reverend Wada were discouraged by the dirt and junk left by war workers who had lived in the house while the Japanese were away. The roomers hadn't cared much about the house, because for them it was only a place to spend a few months and then move on.

Yuki looked around her room now, wondering if maybe this was the very room where old Mr. Toda had once lived long ago when the house first became a dormitory for the young men from Japan. He had often told her how it was in those early days, and she tried now to think of Mr. Toda as he might have been then, his hair still black, his back straight and his legs strong.

Maybe it was from this very room he had gone to clean windows or scrub floors or wash dishes in some dingy cafe, or, in the season of the summer fruit, he'd gone to the valleys to pick peaches and cherries and apricots in the scorching sun with the other young men.

Mr. Toda had told her how, when the rains came, they returned to this house and it was here waiting for them, a refuge in lonely times when they longed for a friendly Japanese face or a bowl of hot bean paste soup. Over the years most of the men had sent to Japan for wives and moved away. But Mr. Toda hadn't. Like a bird that never left its first nest, he had stayed, perhaps in this very room, Yuki thought, until the army had sent him off to the desert in Utah.

Yuki wrinkled her nose as she looked at the walls streaked by leaking rain and spattered with grease behind the small table ringed with burn marks.

Limp, ragged curtains hid the dirty window panes and a green window shade lay askew on the floor, exactly where it had fallen. Dust balls stirred lazily as

Yuki walked around the room, and dust covered the cardboard cartons full of empty cans, beer bottles and food cartons encrusted still with bits of gray-green mold.

"Ugh!" Yuki sniffed.

For a minute even the church balcony with the Wada children seemed better than this mess. But when she thought of Emi and her grandma, she knew the room had to be cleaned. She took a deep breath, held it as long as she could and began to sweep the floor, flinging the dust out into the small, dark hallway.

"*Kora, kora!* Don't sweep all your dust into my room!" Mr. Oka called from the room across the hall.

"Oh, I'm sorry. I didn't know anyone else was living up here."

"Well, it was either here or join the children's brigade in the church balcony, and you wouldn't have wanted me and Hokusai up there, would you?"

"Oh no," Yuki blurted out before she realized how unfriendly that sounded. But the old man hadn't noticed.

"My room's filthy," she explained.

The old man swept past her to see for himself. "Hmmpf," he grunted. "You just need to get rid of all this junk."

And without waiting to be asked, he gathered up an armful of cartons and carted them down the steep steps, while Yuki ran after him picking up the cans and bottles he dropped along the way.

Back upstairs, Mr. Oka poured a generous amount of disinfectant into a bucket of hot soapy water and gave Yuki one of the rags he'd wrung out in it.

60

"The only way to get a room clean," he instructed, "is to start scrubbing. Now let's get to work. I wasn't a houseboy for twenty years for nothing."

"I thought you owned a grocery store," Yuki interrupted.

"I did. But how do you think I saved enough money to buy it in the first place?"

The old man held up his arms and flexed his muscles. "I scrubbed floors and windows like everybody else. I did it in Chicago too when I first got out of camp."

The old man stopped to light a cigarette and then grinned as though he were enjoying a small private joke of his own.

"I swore I'd never scrub another floor for anybody once I got back to California," he said, "and now look at me!"

Yuki didn't know what to say. But the old man went right on as though he were talking to himself.

Then he turned to look at her. "That's all right, little one," he said, blowing a cloud of smoke into the room. "Don't worry. This time I'm doing it because I want to. And that makes a big difference. You can call me Uncle Oka, if you like."

Yuki grinned back at him. "Okay, Uncle Oka." She still didn't quite understand this brusque old man, but she was beginning to like him.

It was the sound of a car driving into the yard and honking wildly that brought them all running outside. Papa first, then Mama and Mrs. Wada, wiping their hands on their aprons, Yuki, thudding down the narrow stairway, and even the Reverend Wada who hurried down the ladder from the church tower where he was hanging an enormous American flag.

"Mrs. Jamieson! Mimi! Mr. Nelson! Mrs. Nelson!" Yuki called out to each of them as they stepped out of the car carrying brooms and buckets and mops and rags.

"We came to help. Can you use some help?"

"We sure can!"

"Come in, come in."

There was such a commotion of greeting and hugging, with the Wada children screaming and running around everybody, that Yuki didn't even notice Mr. Oka hadn't come down. It was only when they all sat down to eat the fried chicken and potato salad Mrs. Nelson brought for lunch that he finally came downstairs, and only after he was called twice. Then he sat at the end of the table and hardly said a word to anyone.

Yuki saw Mrs. Jamieson try to have a conversation with him.

"Would you care for more chicken, Mr. Oka?" she asked. "Did you enjoy the potato salad?"

But Mr. Oka pretended he couldn't speak English, only nodding or shaking his head in answer to her questions, so he wouldn't have to talk to her.

After lunch when they all got to work and Mimi came upstairs to help Yuki finish cleaning her room, Mr. Oka vanished altogether.

Mimi stood in front of the mirror in Yuki's room running a comb through her long blond hair. She was looking at herself, but she spoke of Mr. Oka.

"That old man's a strange character," she remarked with a frown. "I don't think I like him much."

Yuki found herself defending him.

"He's okay when you get to know him," she said loyally, "He's just sort of different."

Mimi shrugged. "Oh well, I don't really care," she said, and taking one last look at herself, she asked, "Did I ever write you about the new boy in class? He's got the bluest eyes I've ever seen."

That night at supper Yuki asked Mr. Oka where he'd been all afternoon. Without waiting for an answer she asked, "Didn't you like my friends?"

Mr. Oka thought for a moment. "They were all right for white folks, I guess," he said lightly, and Yuki could tell he didn't care a lot about them.

"Mimi was my best friend at school," she explained. But even as she said so, she knew Mimi was different. There was a space between them now, and it was hard to say why. Yuki just knew it was Emi now who was her best friend.

"Well, you'll like Emi and her grandma," she promised. "And I know you'll like Mr. Toda."

"Will I?"

"Sure, you just wait and see if you don't. And I know for positive sure you'll like my brother Ken. He was wounded in France, but he's getting therapy for his leg in an army hospital in Washington now. He'll be home pretty soon too."

Then the gathering would be complete. They'd all be together in a nice house Papa would find for them, and the days of waiting and longing would be over.

"Hey, Uncle Oka," Yuki said, "maybe if I just will it to happen, they might all be back next week, even Ken. Wouldn't that be super colossal?"

Uncle Oka nodded. "It could happen."

Maybe it could. Maybe it really could. A surge of joy streaked through Yuki, making her want to shout at the whole world.

"Yahoooo!" she sang out, causing Hokusai to let out a terrible screech, leap from Uncle Oka's arms and escape down the dark hallway.

Suddenly the dingy room seemed too small to hold her bursting spirits. Yuki rushed downstairs and outside where the Wada children were whooping and hollering around a roaring trash fire.

"Hey, maybe they'll all be back next week," she shouted into their hot, glowing faces.

They didn't know what Yuki was talking about, but they jumped up and down and clapped their hands and danced around the blazing fire with her, as though she'd just told them the war had come to an end.

9

"WE'RE COMING! WE'RE COMING!" EMI WROTE. SHE SENT Yuki the time and date their train would arrive, and underlined everything three times. "See you SOON," she scribbled all around the border of the page.

There were cots in all the rooms of the old house behind the church now, and it was ready for the Japanese who were coming home from the camps. Students from the campus church had come with ladders and brushes and buckets of paint and made the walls the color of pale sunshine. They sang as they worked, making the house echo with friendly sounds, and when they'd finished, it was as though the old house had been roused from a long, dark sleep. Yuki hardly recognized her room with its fresh coat of paint and new curtains at the window, and now there were two cots beside her own, for Emi and her grandma.

"What time does their train come in?" Yuki asked Papa for the third time since lunch.

"It's still the same, Yuki, four twenty. They're an hour late."

In two hours and fifteen minutes and forty-five seconds they'd be here. Yuki ran upstairs and inspected everything once more. Mama had helped her put fresh linen and blankets on the two extra cots just that morning, and now Yuki brushed a hand over each of them, smoothing out every small wrinkle she saw. She admired again the big sign she'd made out of cardboard with the bright crayon lettering, "Welcome home, Emi and Grandma Kurihara." She added a few flowers and curlecues and stars around the sign for Mr. Toda and put it on his cot in the room he would share with Mr. Oka. Then she was ready. It was time to go to the station.

The last few minutes of waiting were always the hardest. Yuki looked down the tracks dozens of times while Papa talked to the man from the mortuary who would take Grandpa Kurihara's coffin from the train. Finally she saw the engine chuffing toward her, pulling the train over the same hundreds of miles she'd traveled herself, gliding over the rails that wound over deserts and plains like a pair of shiny snakes.

"Here it comes, Papa. Here it comes."

The train pulled into the station, hissing and grinding to a slow stop. Yuki ran along side, trying to find Emi among the blurred faces peering from inside.

"Papa, suppose they aren't on the train?" Yuki began. "Suppose the bus from Topaz didn't get to the station in time and they missed it? Suppose there was an awful dust storm just when they were leaving and . . ."

"Yuki, will you please stop." And then Papa said, "There they are!"

He was right. It was Emi wearing the red dress her grandma had made for her when they were in Camp Topaz. There was her short, plump grandma behind her, moving slowly and carefully. She was carrying so many bundles and packages, she could barely hold onto the handrail.

"Emi! Grandma Kurihara! Here we are. Over here . . . over here." Yuki darted in and out among the other waiting people, calling out as she ran.

It wasn't until she'd hugged them both that Yuki noticed how sad they looked.

"Where's Mr. Toda? Is he still on the train?"

Emi shook her head, but said nothing. Her grandmother bit her lip and looked at Papa with a sad, puzzled expression.

"Didn't you get the telegram from Topaz?" she asked.

"Yes, the one confirming your arrival time."

"No, no," Grandma Kurihara said, grasping Papa's arm now to make sure he understood. "The second telegram."

It was Papa who was puzzled now. "A second telegram? Why, no."

Grandma Kurihara began to dab at her eyes with a rumpled handkerchief. "Then you don't know? How can I tell you? It was all so sad and sudden and terrible," she said, sobbing. "He was so looking forward to coming home."

Papa spoke gently to her. "Now, Mrs. Kurihara, please pull yourself together. What is it? Where is Mr. Toda? Has something happened to him?"

She nodded, sniffing. "We brought back two coffins on this train, instead of just one."

Yuki turned toward the baggage car and saw one pine coffin being lifted out and then another right behind it. One was Grandpa Kurihara's and the second had to be Mr. Toda's.

But how could Mr. Toda be dead? Just last week he had sent Mama his latest poem. "My leaping heart is home with you now ... The frail body hastens to follow." Had his spirit come home then because it couldn't wait for his tired body? Had he known perhaps that he was going to die? Yuki shivered as though a cold wind had suddenly filtered through her soul.

Emi whispered to her. "They said he was too excited about coming back. He was standing in line for supper at the mess hall and he crumpled up like a heap of rags. His heart just stopped beating."

Yuki nodded. There was nothing she could say.

Mama wept when they told her, but she soon wiped her eyes and said, "We mustn't grieve too much. We should be happy that Grandpa Kurihara and Mr. Toda are together now, and they'll never be sad or lonely or afraid again."

Still Yuki didn't think it was fair. They had both wanted so badly to come home to California. Instead, they'd both died in the lonely desert concentration

camp a long way from home. She ran upstairs to get the welcome sign she'd made for Mr. Toda. She tore it into small pieces and flung it into the trash can.

"It's not fair," she murmured.

Emi watched, her wide eyes dark and glistening. "People have to die," she said slowly. "And you have to let them go. That's what Grandma told me when my mama and papa died. She said the ones left behind have to be strong and keep on living."

Yuki was surprised how old and wise Emi sounded. Emi seemed to understand certain things far better than she ever could. Still, Yuki couldn't quite let Mr. Toda go. She had a lingering feeling of anger and loss because he had been taken from her so suddenly.

The next morning the Reverend Wada held a brief funeral service for the two men in the chapel. Mrs. Wada removed the covering from the reed organ and played "Nearer My God to Thee," and Papa said a few words in memory of the two men.

But Yuki wasn't listening. Instead, she remembered how Mr. Toda had been such an important part of her life ever since she could remember.

As Yuki listened to Papa's words drifting over her head, she sent one last message to Mr. Toda. "Be sure you link up with Mrs. Jamieson's captain out there, wherever you are," she said. "And look for Pepper too. Good-bye now, Mr. Toda. Good-bye forever."

By the time they got to the cemetery, a light rain had begun to fall. It shrouded the living as well as the dead, covering everything with hazy gray mist. Yuki held on to Emi's hand as they walked carefully over the wet grass, weaving in and out, so they wouldn't walk on the heads and stomachs of the people buried there. And when the graveside service was over, they all walked down the gentle slope of the road as Mama led them toward Hana's grave. She was the first one to notice and gave a small cry of anguish.

"What is it, Mama?"

"Hana Chan's flowering cherry tree. Look what someone's done to it!"

It had been chopped down and lay on the ground lifeless, its leaves withered and dead.

"Who could have done such a thing?" Grandma Kurihara wondered as she bent to touch the wounded place where the tree had been cut. "Someone who still hates us?"

No one answered her.

Papa picked up the dead tree and carried it to the trunk of the car. "We can put it up in the church yard and tie some bread on it for the birds," he said gently. "You'd like that wouldn't you, Mama?"

Mama could only nod. "That would be nice," she murmured after a few moments. "And we can plant another tree for Hana so it will bloom again next spring."

They went away quickly then, leaving the dead to rest peacefully in the quiet gray rain.

Yuki and Emi helped Papa plant the dead cherry tree and tie pieces of bread and suet on its branches for the birds. Yuki stepped back to admire the tree. It almost looked like a Christmas tree bearing gifts of bread for the birds.

Hana would like it, she thought. So would Mr. Toda. And for a moment it was almost as though they were both right there looking at the tree too.

Suddenly Yuki felt better. She no longer felt so bad about never seeing Mr. Toda again. It was all right, she told herself. He had come home after all.

CHAPTER

10

ON MONDAY GRANDMA KURIHARA HAD A VISITOR. HE WAS
a tall, heavy man, pale and nervous, wearing a black
suit that seemed too large for him. She called him
Sensei and bowed many times before she hurried to
make some persimmon-leaf tea for him.

"That's the priest from the Buddhist Temple," Emi
whispered.

"Really?" Yuki was surprised. Somehow she expected a priest to be wearing a white robe and carrying
prayer beads in his hands. "He looks just like anybody
else," she observed.

"Sure, but he's special," Emi explained. "Grandma
said so."

The news this special man brought, however, was
not good at all.

"I'm afraid I have some very bad news," he said

to Grandma Kurihara, spacing his words carefully because they were so hard for him to say. "Our temple was vandalized while we were away in camp, and the things you and the others stored in the basement . . . well . . . it was one of those unfortunate things. Someone broke in. The caretaker has fled. We have lost everything. It is all gone."

Grandma Kurihara's lips quivered. "Everything? My trunks with my valuables? My Satsuma plates and my husband's collection of sword guards? Our photograph albums and our good clothes?" She was naming her possessions one by one. "My refrigerator and stove too?"

The priest wiped his face with a large white handkerchief and his fingers moved nervously, as though seeking his prayer beads.

"I am so sorry," he said over and over, "but there is nothing to be done. I hear there are many others who lost what they thought was safely stored. Farmers have returned to find their orchards withered from lack of care. Nurserymen have come back to dead plants and shattered greenhouses. Promises have been broken and trusts betrayed."

Grandma rocked back and forth in her chair, sighing and moaning. "But what am I to do? All my grandchild and I have left now are the four suitcases we carried with us into camp."

The priest tried to comfort her. "I promise to do whatever I can to help you," he assured her.

But when he left, Grandma Kurihara murmured, "What can one man do? What can anybody do?"

"We must all help each other now," Papa said, trying to make her feel better. But Papa was having his own troubles too.

"Nobody seems to want to hire an enemy alien on parole," he said gloomily. "And all the jobs and houses have been taken by defense workers who moved here while we were gone."

Mama tried to cheer him up. "The war will end soon, Papa," she consoled. "You said yourself Japan can't go on fighting much longer. And when the war ends, you won't be an enemy alien anymore."

Mama was right. The war did end soon after, when the United States dropped atomic bombs on Hiroshima and Nagasaki.

Yuki and Emi were listening to the radio when they heard the announcement that Japan had accepted the terms of the United States and had surrendered.

"Hey, Japan's surrendered! The war's over!"

They ran downstairs, shouting to anybody who was around to listen. They almost stumbled over Mr. Oka sitting on the front steps holding Hokusai in his lap.

"Uncle Oka, have you heard? The war's over!"

"Japan finally gave up," Emi said, bending over to speak into his good ear. "The war's over!"

"I know," Uncle Oka said without looking up. "I heard."

"Then why do you look so sad? Aren't you glad?"

Uncle Oka looked up at last. "How can I be glad when my brothers and their families were burned to death by that monstrous atomic bomb?"

Yuki gasped. "They lived in Hiroshima, Uncle Oka?"

The old man nodded. "There were beautiful green fields of rice around my father's house," he said, remembering a time long past. "When I was small I could hide in them for hours and no one could find me except the crows that wheeled around the sun in the bright summer sky."

It was as though all the years of Uncle Oka's life were coming together before his eyes, and in the same instant, he knew that everything was lost forever.

Yuki and Emi sat down beside him trying to share his grief, and the Japanese part of each of them understood his sadness. Yuki reached for his cat and rubbed the silky softness of its throat until it began to purr. She hoped Uncle Oka understood that she was telling him she cared about him too.

"Ah well," he sighed at last. "In war nobody wins. Nobody at all."

When Mrs. Jamieson heard of the surrender, she went straight to her kitchen, put on her apron, and baked her best sour cream coffee cake. Then she called a taxi and told the driver to rush her to the Japanese church. When she arrived, she found Yuki and Emi still sitting with Mr. Oka on the steps of the house in back.

She looked at them, and for the first time in her life, she seemed to have run out of words. She dabbed at her eyes with a lacy blue handkerchief and then thrust the cake at Mr. Oka.

"What can I say?" she asked. "Whenever I have no words to say what is in my heart, I bake a cake and just hope it somehow carries all the thoughts I cannot seem to speak."

The old man nodded briefly, but no one knew whether he understood what she was trying to say.

Mrs. Jamieson thought how his heart must ache for his homeland and the family he'd lost. She imagined, too, that for Yuki's mother and father there was joy that peace had come to the two countries they loved. But through that happiness there probably ran a deep current of sadness for those they had left behind in Japan. She brushed her hands together now, as though disposing of her private thoughts. "Well, at last your mama and papa are no longer 'enemy aliens,' Yuki."

"Thank goodness," Yuki agreed. She'd always hated their being called enemies, as though the war had suddenly made them different people when they'd always been the same caring people who loved America just as they loved Japan.

Mrs. Jamieson shook a ringed finger at her. "And just you wait. One of these days our country will pass a law so they can become citizens too, just like anybody else. Imagine," she said to Mr. Oka, as though he weren't aware of it, "having a law that keeps all Asian people from becoming citizens. Such utter nonsense!"

She was getting stirred up now as she always did when she thought of life's injustices. And as though she couldn't waste another minute, she hurried inside to see Yuki's mother and father. After she'd talked to them, she spoke again to Yuki.

"I'm going right home and write to President Truman," she said with a determined look. "It's time we changed a lot of things in this country."

Then she rushed as fast as her lame leg would allow to the waiting taxi, and as quickly as she had come, Mrs. Jamieson was gone.

The end of the war brought many changes to life at the hostel, for now all the Japanese in the camps were being sent back to California. Each day more and more of them arrived, tired and worn, carrying bulging bundles and dusty suitcases, worried and anxious about beginning their lives over again. There were army cots everywhere now—in the halls and classrooms of the church and in every room of the house in back.

"Golly, I'm beginning to feel like I'm back in camp again," Emi complained, as she and Yuki stood waiting to get into the bathroom.

"Me too," Yuki sighed. "What'll we do if the people just keep on coming?"

"Escape someplace, I guess."

"But where?"

That was the problem. There was nowhere for them to go.

One morning Papa lingered at the breakfast table for a second cup of coffee and Mama came from the kitchen to join him.

"I think it's time for us to move out and make room for the newcomers from camp, Mama."

"I was thinking the same thing," she answered, nodding. "But where can we go?"

Papa beckoned to Mr. Oka and told Emi to go call her grandma. As soon as Grandma Kurihara arrived he said, "I've had this idea spinning around in my head for some time now. We all need work and a place to live. We each have some money but not enough to start alone. So it makes sense for us to pool our resources and go into business together, doesn't it?"

Uncle Oka poured three heaping spoonfuls of sugar into his coffee and stirred it slowly. "If I'm thinking what you're thinking, I say maybe you are a little bit crazy, but also very wonderful." He looked at Papa hopefully. "What kind of business were you thinking of?"

Papa grinned. "The same one you were, Mr. Oka."

Grandma Kurihara fidgeted nervously in her chair. "I wish you gentlemen would stop talking in riddles and tell this old lady what it is that's whirling around in your heads."

But Mama had guessed. "If I'm not mistaken, I think they're speaking of Mr. Oka's Sunshine Grocery. Am I right?"

"That's it exactly," Papa admitted. "Then Mr. Oka could have his old store back, and Mrs. Kurihara, you and your husband owned a grocery store before the war, didn't you? Well, we could make good use of your experience now. And my job would be to keep the books and do the paperwork."

"That'd be super," Yuki began. But Papa wasn't finished.

"If we can raise five thousand dollars in cash for the stock and the fixtures in the shop and take over the lease, the shop is ours. And the best part is," he added with a wide smile, "there's an apartment above the shop with three bedrooms."

Everybody began to talk at once. Uncle Oka and Papa began to scribble on some paper, figuring what each of them could contribute. But Grandma Kurihara suddenly rose and left the room.

"Grandma!" Emi called after her. "Where're you going? Don't you want to be part of the shop?"

Mama looked disappointed. "Maybe she needs a little time to think about it, Emi. After all, she's had her heart set on buying back her own shop in San Francisco for a long time."

"But it won't be any fun without Grandma Kurihara and Emi," Yuki said dismally. Why did Emi's grandma have to be so difficult?

But in a few minutes, the old woman came pattering down the stairs, almost losing the zoris on her feet in her rush. She sat down beside Papa and placed in front of him a small purple satin pouch, drawn together with a black silk cord.

"There," she said with a pleased look. "I had that hidden in the toe of my Sunday shoes."

Papa opened the pouch and counted the wad of neatly folded bills he found inside. It was not a very large amount, but he knew it was all the money Grandma Kurihara had in the world.

"Thank you very much, Mrs. Kurihara," he said with a bow. "Yours is the first contribution to our new business."

Mr. Oka drew in his breath and pounded on the

80

table like an auctioneer. "Done!" he said. "We're in business. The Sakane-Oka-Kurihara partnership has begun."

And they all shook hands on it. Even Yuki and Emi.

"Now we can all live together above the shop," Yuki announced, sounding like Emi's grandma taking charge.

She heard Uncle Oka mutter, "Not me, I'm staying here." But she really didn't mind. Emi and Grandma Kurihara would be coming with them, and they were moving out of the hostel to something like a home, even if it was only an apartment above a grocery store.

Mama and Papa were talking eagerly with Mr. Oka and Emi's grandma now. They were laughing together, and they sounded different because their voices held at last the bright sound of hope.

YUKI AND EMI STOOD IN FRONT OF THE STORE, THEIR heads tipped back, squinting up at the big new sign Papa and Uncle Oka had put up. "People's Grocery," it read, and in the window there was a sign that said, "Everybody welcome."

"This is a lot nicer than Grandma's old store," Emi said, admiring the store's fresh coat of paint. It was the color of apples leaves, and she touched it now with the tip of her finger to see if it was dry.

"Uncle Oka says it looks ten times better than when he had it before the war." Yuki took a few steps back to get a better look and bumped into a tall man standing near the curb. He was in work clothes and carried a black lunch pail as though he were just going to work. Neither of them had noticed him as he stood there listening to them admire the shop.

"You people taking over?" he asked. His voice was flat and controlled. It had no hint of either friendliness or hate. He wasn't smiling, but he wasn't frowning either.

Yuki looked at his hard blue eyes. "My papa and his friends just bought it," she answered proudly. "It's going to be the best grocery store around here."

Yuki smiled at him and was immediately sorry, for the man didn't smile back. He closed himself off, making her feel small and worthless. She stopped talking, but now Emi spoke up.

"My grandma is going to help run it too."

The man simply listened and turned the same expressionless look toward Emi. He acted, in fact, as though Yuki and Emi weren't even there. He seemed to have important and private thoughts in his head that had nothing whatever to do with them.

"I see," he said at last, and then walked quickly away from them down the street.

Emi shrugged. "He's weird."

"He sure is. He gives me the creeps."

They turned back then to admiring the store and didn't give him another thought.

While Yuki's mother and father worked to get settled in the apartment upstairs, Grandma Kurihara and Uncle Oka ran the store downstairs. The two of them were like a dog and cat, watching each other warily, neither one quite certain what to make of the other.

Uncle Oka wasn't sure how to handle the talkative old woman who wanted to be in charge. "Doesn't she know that I, Kunisaburo Oka, ran this very store for fifteen years before the war?' he grumbled to Yuki. "Doesn't she know I don't need a bossy old woman to tell me how to run my business?"

And Grandma Kurihara on her part would complain to Emi about having the old man underfoot all the time. It was a good thing, she said, that he was staying at the hostel and not living with them in the apartment.

"Don't you like him, Grandma?" Emi asked.

"Well, I suppose he is clever about getting the best produce at the best prices," she admitted. "And he does work hard, going down to the wholesale market to buy it every morning at four o'clock."

That was about as close as she came to saying anything nice about him. Still, when she felt the need to go to the cemetery and talk to Grandpa Kurihara on a Sunday afternoon, it was usually Uncle Oka who took her there in the battered truck he'd bought. Grandma would murmur her *Namu Amida Butsu* beside Grandpa's grave. Then, sometimes, she would produce two cold sausages and some bread from her bulging handbag, and the two of them would sit in the truck and have a snack beside the slope of the grave-dotted grass.

Sometimes Mama worried that Mr. Oka and Grandma Kurihara weren't getting along in the shop. But Papa said they were doing fine, and he spent most of his time upstairs unpacking their belongings. All the things they'd packed in such a hurry now began coming out of storage and friends' basements and attics, like long-lost children coming home. Papa didn't think they should get everything at once, but Mama was anxious to live again with her own things. "I want to sit in my old rocker," she explained, "and use my sewing machine and have all my books around me again even if I don't have time to read them."

The apartment soon became an impossible jumble of furniture and cartons and packing boxes, and it almost seemed like those frantic days when the army had given them ten days to get out. But this time they were unpacking all the familiar objects of their past life. It was like being propelled backward through time, and Yuki felt as though she were seeing small pieces of her old self coming out of each carton.

"Hey, Emi, look. Here's my old Orphan Annie mug. And here're my old diaries and my box of beads, and wait a minute, I'm going to look for Mrs. Jamieson's pearl ring."

Yuki waded through the crumpled newspapers that came billowing out of the cartons and went to look inside Mama's big brown trunk that had been in storage. She knew exactly where to look, and she found the small black velvet box she'd hidden inside a pair of red socks. She lifted the gold ring from its white satin nest and held it out for Emi to see.

"Oooooh, it's beautiful. Why don't you wear it to church on Sunday?"

Yuki shook her head. "I'm saving it."

"What for? Your wedding day?"

"Not for *that* long. I told Mrs. Jamieson I'd wear it to celebrate when we were back home once more."

"Well, you're home now, aren't you?"

"Not really. I'm waiting till we move back to a real house."

"Oh."

Yuki didn't notice the disappointment in Emi's voice. She was rummaging about in another carton now and pulled out one of Ken's old records. "This was Ken's favorite," she said, and as she put the record on the player the slow sweet strains of Glenn Gray's orchestra filled the room. "I will gather stars out of the blue . . . for you . . . for you . . ."

Suddenly, Yuki had the most terrible longing to see Ken again. "I wonder when he's ever coming home?" she murmured.

"Probably not till the doctors are good and ready to let him go," Emi answered dismally.

Ken was still in the army hospital in Washington, but as far as Yuki was concerned, he might just as well have been in France.

"I guess you're right," she said with a sigh. "I guess he won't be home for a long time yet." And she put the record away carefully into its jacket and pushed it back into the carton of Ken's belongings.

For Yuki, one of the best things to come out of storage was her own bed and mattress with the curves and lumps in just the right places. It felt wonderful to curl up in it again, as though her body had found its old nest.

Papa put a rollaway bed in Yuki's room for Emi, and the two of them whispered and giggled and talked every night until Mama or Papa rapped on the walls and told them to go to sleep.

One night Emi whispered in the darkness. "Where will your brother sleep when he comes home?"

Yuki guessed Emi was worried that she and her grandma would have to move out when Ken came home. She had worried about that herself, but now it seemed perfectly simple. "Ken can sleep on the sofa in the living room," she answered. "He won't mind. You'll see. You won't have to move out."

"Thank goodness." Emi sighed.

"Don't worry," Yuki whispered. "We'll take care of you forever."

But Emi didn't hear her. She had already fallen asleep.

It was Grandma Kurihara's urgent shouting that woke them up with a start. It was only six o'clock, but she had already gone down to the shop. Almost immediately, she had rushed back upstairs, gasping and shouting.

"Fire! Help! Fire! Come quickly, Mr. Sakane."

Yuki tried to shake the sleep from her eyes, wondering if she were having another nightmare. But now she heard the sound of pounding feet as Papa rushed downstairs. And then Mama hurried into their room.

"Wake up, girls! Quickly! We've got to get out of the apartment. There's a fire downstairs. Hurry!"

This wasn't a nightmare. This was real. Already Yuki could see and smell the thin wisps of smoke that filtered upstairs. They rushed down into the shop where Papa and Grandma Kurihara were trying frantically to put out the smoldering fire. The shop soon filled with thick black smoke that stung at their eyes and made them cough.

"Yuki, run next door and call the fire department," Papa shouted.

"Hurry!" Mama called after her.

Yuki had never even noticed who lived next door in the old two-storied frame house. She ran there now with Emi close behind her. She pushed heavily on the doorbell while Emi pounded on the door.

"Help! Fire! Hurry!" they shouted together.

Finally a sleepy-looking man in a rumpled bathrobe came shuffling to the door. "What is it?" he asked.

"Fire!" Yuki shouted at him. "Call the fire department."

"Hurry!" Emi screamed. "Our store's on fire."

The man was wide awake now. He ran to the phone and in a few minutes they heard the shrill wail of the siren as the fire engine came tearing down the street.

CHAPTER

12

THEY ALL STOOD OUTSIDE THE SHOP WATCHING HELP-lessly as the black smoke billowed and writhed like an angry dragon and rushed out at them, making them cough and back away. Grandma Kurihara dabbed at her eyes with a big handkerchief, and Yuki wasn't sure if it was because of the smoke or because she was crying.

"They tried to destroy us," she said bitterly.

"Who, Mrs. Kurihara?" Papa asked urgently. "Did you see them?"

She shook her head. "I only heard the crash of the glass and smelled gasoline. Then when I saw the fire start I ran upstairs to call you."

The firemen put out the blaze quickly, pouring great streams of water on the shooting flames. They checked carefully to make sure the last spark was out, and they also checked the apartment upstairs.

The chief came to talk to Papa and listen to Grandma Kurihara's story. "I'm sorry it happened, Mr. Sakane," he said. "There are some who think they still have to fight the war against Japan right here. It's ridiculous, but it's happening." He wiped his face and pushed back his hat. "I'm just glad we caught it before you lost the whole building."

Papa thanked him and shook his hand. Then they all went in to see what was left of the store. The front window was shattered where a brick had been thrown. There was broken glass everywhere, and the whole store was flooded with water. Smoke had blackened the walls, most of the shelves were charred, and the counter was a black hulk of burned wood. Labels had been burned or washed off most of the canned goods and everything that wasn't in tins or bottles was useless.

"Oh Papa," Mama sighed. "Have we lost everything?"

Before Papa could answer, Mr. Oka came rumbling back from the wholesale market where he'd gone to get the day's produce. He rushed into the store shouting, "What's happened? What's happened? What's become of our store?" His eyes were glittering and his forehead was damp with sweat.

When Papa told him, Mr. Oka's shoulders sagged as though someone had put a bundle on his back that was too heavy for him to carry. He walked aimlessly around the store, kicking at the broken glass and the cans that had tumbled from the shelves. The veins at his temples were throbbing and his fists were clenched tight.

Suddenly he began to shout, "They aren't going to put me out of business again! They aren't! They aren't!"

Papa put a hand on his shoulder. "You're right, Mr. Oka. We're not going to let anybody force us to give up."

Yuki wondered why anyone would want to destroy their one small grocery store. What harm were they doing here? Who would do such a thing anyway?

And then Yuki looked up and saw again the man with the cold blue eyes who'd asked about their store. He peered briefly into the store, his eyes met Yuki's for only a moment, and then he walked quickly away.

Was he the one? Had he come back to see how much damage he'd done? Yuki felt a rush of anger boil up inside. But she also felt afraid, and she didn't like the sick feeling she had in the pit of her stomach. She hated it. Suddenly she found herself crying, and quickly she wiped away the tears with the back of her hand so no one would see her.

A small crowd of people gathered around the store now to see what the excitement was about. Mostly they were curious, but a few came inside to tell them they were sorry.

"It's a shame," one woman said, her voice touched with sympathy. "You'll open again, won't you?"

Then Yuki noticed the man from next door. She barely recognized him now that he was dressed in a plaid shirt and a pair of faded overalls. His sand-colored hair was thinning at the top, like Papa's, and his gray eyes were kind. He had an open face that seemed to reveal exactly what he was feeling.

He came straight to Yuki and asked if she was all right. He gave her a light pat on the shoulder to show that he cared. Then he turned to Papa. "Have you people had breakfast?" he asked. "My wife says for you all to come over and have some hot coffee and rolls."

"Ah, that's very kind of you." Mama and Papa murmured their thanks together.

"You must be cold," the man said.

It was only then that Yuki realized she was barefoot and shivering in her thin bathrobe. A thick gray summer fog still hung over the city and there was no sign yet of the sun breaking through. She looked at Emi and saw that she was shivering too. Her felt slippers were sopping wet, but she didn't even seem to notice. Like Yuki, she was numb. It was as though this whole thing had been a terrible nightmare.

"My name's Stephen Olssen," the neighbor said, as he led them to his house. "We've been meaning to come say hello, and now this . . . It's a shame."

When they were inside their neighbor's house, Yuki noticed something. "Where's Uncle Oka?" she asked.

"He wouldn't come," Papa said in a low voice. "He still has a lot of sorting out to do."

"In the shop?"

Papa shook his head. "No, I'm afraid it's inside his head."

Yuki wasn't sure what Papa meant, but now she couldn't worry any more about Uncle Oka, for Mrs. Olssen came out with a tray that held a pitcher of steaming hot chocolate, a pot of coffee and an enormous platter full of sweet rolls with butter melting over them in thick yellow swirls. Her long brown hair was swept up neatly into a large bun and she wore a blue apron over her skirt and blouse. There was something comfortable and relaxed about her manner that put them all at ease, and Yuki liked her immediately.

"My name's Emma," she began. "I meant to bring over some cookies when you moved in, but well, now you're all here. And I'm so very sorry about the fire."

Her words came out in a friendly stream as she poured cups of steaming coffee and mugs of hot chocolate.

"Now which of you is the older sister?" she asked Emi.

And quiet Emi suddenly began talking as though she'd known Emma Olssen all her life. She quickly told her that she and Yuki weren't sisters at all, and how they came to be living together. Then Mama talked, telling how she had a son who'd been wounded in the war.

"He must be about our Johnny's age," Emma Olssen said softly.

"Ah, you have a son in the army too?" Papa asked.

The smile faded quickly from Mrs. Olssen's face, and she looked to her husband to answer Papa's question.

"No . . . Johnny joined the marines," Stephen Olssen said briefly, and then quickly changing the subject he said, "Say, let me know when you need help repairing your store. I'm a carpenter by trade and I'd like to give you a hand with new shelving or whatever else you need in the store.

Yuki saw Stephen Olssen's strong arms and hands

and felt his strength spilling out to each of them. Papa no longer looked so grim or tense, and Mama and Grandma Kurihara had begun to smile again. Yuki and Emi had both stopped shivering. Emma and Stephen Olssen had not only warmed them with their hot breakfast, their caring seemed to make the terrible thing that had happened a little easier to bear.

Emi's grandmother didn't say much at the Olssens; but when they came back to the store she said thoughtfully, "Well, we may still have a lot of enemies, but we know we have some fine friends too."

Yuki wished Uncle Oka would agree with her. She wanted to tell him about the good feeling she had about their neighbors. But Uncle Oka was busy sweeping out the water and the broken glass and the debris that was all that remained of their grocery store.

"You should have come next door with us," Yuki said eagerly. "The Olssens are really nice."

But the old man shrugged. "They are all the same," he muttered. And he didn't even look up from his work.

CHAPTER

13

YUKI STRETCHED OUT ON THE SUN-DRIED WEEDS SHE'D flattened with her stomach and looked around at the shimmering wheat-colored wall of weeds around her. She heard a slight rustle and the weed wall parted in front of her nose. Uncle Oka's cat stalked silently into her private space and brought her another of its gifts.

"Ugh, Hokusai! Did you bring me another mouse?"

But she reached out to stroke the cat's soft head and drew it close. "I know," she said, "it's a token of your friendship. Okay then, thanks a lot . . . I guess."

Having deposited the gift, the cat slipped away as quickly as it had come. Yuki edged back from the tiny gray corpse and allowed the weeds to hide it from view.

She lay very still then, listening, and wishing

somehow that the little mouse would get up and scurry away. But the only sounds she heard were the sounds of the city.

She flopped over on her back and watched the clouds move across her part of the earth, as though someone were plucking wad after wad of white cotton and flinging them into a wide blue basket. Would they float all the way to Washington, she wondered, across the country and over the army hospital where Ken was getting therapy for his leg?

With Ken closer, it should have been easier to send him her mental messages, but strangely enough, it had become just about impossible. Yuki would close her eyes and try to picture Ken's face with the strong nose and the dark, thick-lashed eyes she coveted so greatly. She held him as close as she could in her mind, but he seemed almost farther away than when he was fighting in France. So now she wrote letters instead of sending messages.

She stuffed two pieces of chewing gum into her mouth, peeled off the letter she'd begun to Ken on her tablet and started over on a new page.

"Dear Ken:" she began.

"I really and truly do wish you would hurry up and come home. It's getting downright boring around here. Rev. Wada's over, but he's helping Mama and Papa. Emi and her grandma went off to visit friends in San Francisco, and here I am lying in the back yard with only a dead mouse for company!

"I'll even be glad when school starts. But I feel kind of scared and creepy about starting at a new school. Suppose nobody will talk to Emi or me? But then maybe that would happen even if I could go back to Jefferson now. Do you think so? I guess maybe Papa was right. He said nothing stays the same. Even Mimi's different."

Yuki shifted her wad of gum to the other cheek and thought about Mimi. Then decided instead to write Ken about their grocery store.

"It really looks neat now that Mr. Olssen helped us build new shelves and a counter," she wrote. "You'll like the Olssens. I like them almost as much as Mrs. Jamieson, and you know that's a lot. Hurry up and come home so you can meet them. And, Ken, write soon. Your ever loving and only sister, Yuki."

Yuki read the letter over and crossed out "write soon." "Answer immediately," she wrote instead. She knew very well, however, that Ken might not even answer her at all.

Ever since he had been sent to the hospital in Washington he hardly ever wrote home. And when he did, his letters just didn't sound like Ken. It was like the time in Topaz when he'd grown so strange and sullen and wouldn't eat with them at their mess hall. Mama had said then it was because he'd lost his freedom and needed to get back out into the world. Maybe what he needed now was to get out of the hospital and the army and come back home.

When he was home Yuki was sure he'd be once more her cheerful, good-looking, six-foot brother, the star forward of the Japanese Men's Club basketball team, who one day was going to become a great doctor.

She wouldn't even mind if he bossed her around a little or ignored her and went off to dances and movies with his girl friends. He could do whatever he pleased, if only he'd just come home.

Mama worried about Ken too. Yuki could see it in her face whenever she read one of Ken's brief letters that only told them he was okay. But Papa reassured her. "He's all right, Mama. They're taking good care of him at the hospital."

And Mama would answer, "I know they're helping him with his leg. It's what's going on inside his head that I'm worried about."

And then one day the telephone rang and Yuki answered it.

"Hello?"

Silence.

"Who is it?"

Then a voice so low she could hardly hear. "Yuki?"

"Who *is* it?"

"Yuki, I'm back."

"Ken? Is it you, Ken? Ken?" Yuki was screaming now.

"Simmer down, Yuki. I'm at the station. I'll be home in a little while."

"Wait . . . I'll call Papa."

"No, don't call him. I'm getting a cab. I don't want anybody to come meet me. Just tell Mom and Pop I'm on my way."

"Ken!" Yuki shrieked, but he'd hung up.

"Mama! Papa! It's Ken. He's home. He's coming home!"

Mama began to cry and raced down to the shop with Yuki to tell Papa.

"If only he'd let us know. Why didn't he let us know he was coming?" Mama said over and over. "Why didn't he want us to meet him at the station? Papa, why are you just standing there? Do something!"

Papa was surprised speechless. "Are you sure it was really Ken?"

Yuki nodded. "I'm sure. I'm sure. He said he was at the station. He's back. He's really back."

Emi was just as excited as Yuki. The two of them squealed and hugged each other and didn't know what to do with themselves. It was as though someone had suddenly told them in July that it would be Christmas that afternoon.

Grandma Kurihara quickly took charge of things. "Well, if your Kenichi is really back, then we must have a celebration," she said scanning the grocery shelves. "Shall we make him some salad with a can of king crab? Or maybe we should open a can of nice tender abalone and slice it with cucumbers. Mr. Oka, do we have some young cucumbers? And maybe a good melon for dessert?"

Mama wondered if she had time to bake a cake before supper, but Mr. Oka was already squeezing his cantaloupes to find one that was just right and brimming with golden juice.

"We'll put a scoop of vanilla ice cream on top," he said. "A son returning from battle certainly deserves our best—especially one who volunteered from behind barbed wire."

"Ah, old man," Grandma Kurihara whispered hoarsely to him. "Must you spill out your bitter thoughts at such a time? This is a day for the Sakanes to be happy and proud."

The old man shrugged. "I know . . . I know . . . leave me be, old woman."

And then Yuki heard the taxi pull up in front of the store, and there was Ken in his uniform, with the 442nd insignia on his sleeve and the bright strip of campaign ribbons on his chest. He got out of the cab slowly, and then they all saw that he was using crutches.

Yuki knew that the shrapnel had shattered his leg. But she thought when he came home from the hospital, he would come home walking straight and tall, his leg healed and strong. It had never once occurred to her that he would come hobbling home on crutches. The pale, thin soldier she saw now didn't really seem to be her brother Ken.

Still, Yuki was the first to fling herself out the door and throw her arms around his neck.

"Ken!" she shouted, her heart about to burst. "You're home! You're really home!"

Ken hugged her back. "Some basketball player I'm gonna be, huh?" he asked softly.

14

~~~~~~~~

THERE WERE A MILLION THINGS YUKI WANTED TO ASK
Ken, and yet now that he was right there, sitting across
the table from her, she couldn't seem to think of a single
thing. Instead she just stared at him, knowing that
something was different. There were creases fanning
out from the corners of his eyes now, and he was so
thin she could see his pale skin stretched taut over the
bones of his cheeks and his jaw.

She saw him shift uncomfortably in his chair and
use his hands to move his right leg when it grew stiff.

"Does it hurt?" she asked at last.

"Not really," Ken answered.

Mama quickly changed the subject. She didn't
want anyone to remind Ken of this terrible thing that
had happened to him that might cripple him for the
rest of his life. She was trying hard only to talk of

pleasant things. With Papa helping, she told about the Henleys in Salt Lake City, and about how they had all bought the store together, and how good it was to have their belongings out of storage at last.

Ken listened, but he wasn't really listening. And he was so quiet, it was almost as though he were sitting there inside a glass cage. They could see him and he could see them, but somehow, they weren't connecting.

Yuki thought of the times when Ken had hardly ever stopped talking and would make her laugh until her sides ached. But Ken's bright, happy self had begun to drain away in camp, and now the fighting and killing in Europe had drained away even more.

Mr. Oka was watching Ken closely. He stretched across the table and offered Ken a cigarette. Ken took it gratefully, let Mr. Oka light it for him and inhaled deeply.

"Maybe now you are sorry you volunteered?" Mr. Oka asked suddenly. It was as though he wanted Ken to spill out his pain and hurt right there in front of them for everyone to see.

Mama gasped and Grandma Kurihara glared at him. "Old man . . ." she began. But Ken didn't seem to mind his asking.

"I'm sorry, but not for the reason you think," he said quietly. "If I had it to do over again, I'd probably volunteer again. But the cost was too high."

Everyone thought Ken was talking about his leg.

"There'll be more therapy, won't there?" Papa asked.

"You'll be able to walk without crutches someday,

won't you?" Yuki blurted out. She didn't see the pained look on Mama's face.

"Maybe," Ken answered slowly. "Maybe I will, and maybe I won't, but . . . well . . . it's only a leg."

Ken had lost more than the use of his leg in the bitter fighting, but he wasn't ready yet to tell them about it. What happened to him was still locked up inside.

Mama understood. "Ken, how about some hot coffee?" she asked, reaching for his cup. She knew Ken was in need of her comfort and her love, but she couldn't take this soldier, her only son, and hold him in her arms as she longed to do. So she offered only what she knew he could accept.

"Thanks, Mom. Some hot coffee would be good."

When Uncle Oka got up and began to look around for Hokusai, Yuki knew he was ready to go home to the hostel. He shook Ken's hand before he left.

"Rest well tonight, Kenichi." Then he let himself out into the night.

Grandma Kurihara wanted to give her room to Ken. "You should have a room to yourself," she insisted.

But Ken insisted just as stubbornly that he was sleeping on the sofa.

At last Grandma Kurihara gave in. "Very well then." She sighed. "But we'll have to talk about making some changes soon."

Yuki knew she was thinking about moving back to the hostel.

"You could move in with Emi and me," she suggested quickly.

106

"Sure," Emi agreed. "We did it before at the hostel. We don't mind your snoring, Grandma."

"Well, we'll have to see," the old woman answered, which at least meant she hadn't made up her mind yet.

Mama and Papa lingered in the living room to fix up the sofa for Ken, tucking in sheets and blankets, fluffing up pillows.

"You're sure you don't mind the sofa?" Mama asked. "We'll borrow a cot for you tomorrow."

"I don't mind, Mom. Honest."

"Well then, have a good rest, Ken. I can't tell you how good it is to have you home."

"I know. Thanks, Mom."

"You're sure you're all right, son? You'll be comfortable?"

"Sure, Pa. I'm fine."

"Good night then. Sleep well. It's good to have you back."

"Thanks. Good night, Pop."

Yuki waited until the night sounds of the apartment had died down. She heard Grandma Kurihara finish in the bathroom. She heard the sounds of Mama and Papa's talking voices grow softer and softer and finally stop altogether. She waited until Emi stopped asking questions about Ken and fell asleep. Then she crept out of bed and tiptoed into the living room.

She could hear the low, even hum of the refrigerator and the ticking of the wall clock as she passed the kitchen. She slipped noiselessly into the living room, tiptoeing as she used to do when she lived above the Henleys. She looked at the sofa and caught her breath.

No one was there. The sheet had been thrown back and there was no sign of Ken.

The light from the street lamp filtered through the shade and Yuki saw Ken sprawled in Papa's armchair, his bad leg thrust out awkwardly in front of him. He was smoking and staring off into space.

"Ken?"

"Hey, you still up, Yuki?"

"Uh-huh. I couldn't sleep."

"Neither could I. Too much excitement, I guess."

"You mean coming home and all?"

Ken didn't answer. He was deep in thought about times and places and happenings that Yuki would never understand or know about. He couldn't even begin to describe them or talk to her about them.

Yuki knew he was far away. She longed for him to get up and put his hand at the back of her neck and march her back to her room the way he used to do when she didn't want to go to bed. She wished he'd throw a pillow at her or poke her in the ribs or wrestle with her on the floor.

But Ken just sat there. She wanted to give him a hug, but there was something about him now that made her draw away.

"Ken?"

"Huh?"

"I'm glad you're back. I really am."

"Good. Thanks. You'd better go back to bed now, Yuki. It's late. Good night."

"G'night, Kenichi Sakane," she said softly, and hurried back to her room.

It wasn't until she was back under the covers that the flood of disappointment hit her. She suddenly realized that there was nothing more to wait and hope for. All these long months, she'd waited and longed for the day when Ken would come home so everything would be wonderful again, the way it was before the war. But now, here he was. Ken was back, and all she felt was empty.

"HE'S GONE!" MAMA SAID, HER VOICE QUIVERING WITH alarm. "He isn't anywhere, and his bag is gone."

Ken had taken off without telling anyone, and no one knew where or why he'd gone. He had been home only for two days and on the third morning, he just disappeared.

Grandma Kurihara shook her head miserably. "Ah . . . ah, you see. It is all my fault. He needed a room of his own. I should have been the one to leave."

"No," Mama said firmly. "It is much more than that. It's something deep inside that's troubling him."

Papa agreed. "If only he could talk about it. If only he could let it out."

Uncle Oka was the only one who said he understood. "Suppose you'd gone off to fight for your country to prove your loyalty and to make it a better place for everyone. Suppose you'd done that and even lost the use of your leg doing it. And then you came home and found restaurants where they wouldn't serve you and barbers who wouldn't cut your hair and shops with 'No Japs' signs in the window. How would you feel? Wouldn't you feel everything you'd done was all for nothing, a total waste?"

No one could answer. Was that it? Was that what was bothering Ken?

At last Papa spoke. "Maybe that's so," he said slowly, "but I don't think that's the kind of ache Ken is feeling now. I think . . . well . . ." Papa's voice drifted off.

"Maybe he's worried about his leg," Yuki suggested.

Emi had another idea. "Maybe it got so bad he went to the Veteran's Hospital in Palo Alto."

"But he'd have told us if that's where he went."

It was a puzzle and no one had an answer. All they could do was wait.

At last Ken telephoned from Merced. He was at the home of his best friend, Jim Hirai.

"Thank goodness," Papa said, relieved. "You two must have a lot to talk about. Have a good time."

"No, Pa, you don't understand. I never wrote you about it, but Jim is dead. It's his family I came to talk to."

"Jim dead?" Papa couldn't believe it.

Jim was Ken's best friend. They had gone through high school together. They were both juniors at the

University when the war broke out. They had worked together at the camp hospital in Topaz, and they had volunteered together when the army came to recruit for an all-Nisei combat unit.

Papa began to understand the shape of Ken's grief.

"I see," he said quietly. "Comfort them as best you can, Ken. And then come on home. We all miss you."

"Thanks, Pa."

"The trip was something Ken had to do," Papa explained. "Maybe now he'll be able to talk to us about it too."

"I hope so," Mama murmured, but she didn't sound very sure.

This time Grandma Kurihara made up her mind. "When Kenichi comes home, he is going to have a room of his own," she announced. "Either I move in with the girls or Emi and I go back to the hostel. Mr. Oka says there is room there now, and it would be simple to move back. After all, Emi and I have only four suitcases to our name."

"You can't go back to the hostel," Yuki insisted.

"And I won't go," Emi said, startling her grandmother.

Emi seemed a little surprised herself for speaking up to her grandmother like that. But after she'd done it once, she did it again. "I'm staying with Yuki," she said firmly.

And for the first time in many years, Grandma gave in to Emi. "Well then," she said amiably, "I guess I move in with you girls."

So now Grandma Kurihara's cot was squeezed in

between Emi and Yuki's beds. The first night she moved in with them, she announced she had a bit of therapy she needed to do on her legs. "Standing all day in the shop doesn't help them one bit," she explained.

"You mean you've got some herb tea for tired legs?" Yuki asked.

"No, not that. Wait and watch. You'll see."

Yuki watched Grandma Kurihara sit on her cot with her legs stretched out in front of her. She had an old candy box beside her, and from it she took a slim stick of incense and lit it. She handed it to Emi. "Here, hold this for me," she instructed.

Next from a wad of the soft burning herb, *moxa*, she took a tiny pinch, smaller than a grain of rice, and licking it lightly so it would stick, she placed it carefully on the muscle of her leg.

"Now," she said to Emi.

Emi bent carefully over it and lit the tiny mound of *moxa* with the incense. The red heat flickered quickly through the *moxa* and burned down to Grandma's leg. The sweet smoky smell of incense and burning *moxa* drifted over them all, and the old woman sucked in her breath.

"*Ah ita, ah ita . . .*" She winced, rocking back and forth at the sharp pain. She sighed with relief when the *moxa* had burned out.

"Why do you do it if it hurts so much?" Yuki asked.

"That's what I say," Emi agreed. "You're crazy, Grandma."

But the old woman looked at them, surprised that they should be so stupid. "It hurts, but it's a good kind

113

of hurt, don't you know. And afterwards, ah, there is such a feeling of relief."

She continued the process over and over again until she'd burned six tiny pinches of *moxa* on each leg.

"It's a counterirritant," she explained. "The sharp pain of the heat makes the dull ache in my leg go away. Want to try? I'll show you."

"No-oo-oo," Yuki and Emi shrieked together.

"That'd be a thousand times worse than eating your essence of egg yolk."

"Or drinking your earthworm brew!"

Emi had already had enough of her grandma's doctoring, and Yuki knew better than to try anything the old woman offered.

That night Grandma Kurihara stayed up whispering and talking with them for a long while. Then she abruptly announced it was time for them to go to sleep. It was hard for Emi and Yuki to go on talking then, for she lay between them looking like a beached whale. When she told them to shush and go to sleep, that's what they had to do.

The night Ken came home from Merced, Grandma talked with them for a long time as they got ready for bed. "He's talking a little more now, did you notice?" she asked.

"But he's still not the same," Yuki observed. "He told Mama today he wasn't going back to college."

"Ever?"

"That's what he said. He said he didn't care whether he became a doctor or not."

"Well, I think he's nice anyway," Emi interrupted. "And he's handsome too."

"Of course he's nice and he's handsome." Grandma sniffed. "But Yuki is right. There is something still troubling him. If we could only find out what it is . . ." Her voice drifted off.

"Emi?" Yuki whispered over the hump that was Grandma.

"What?"

"You still awake?"

"Uh-huh."

"You know what I think? I think . . ."

Grandma Kurihara suddenly sat up in bed. "That's it! I've got it," she said. "What Kenichi needs is a counterirritant to get rid of the ache inside his soul. That's what he needs."

"Oh, Grandma, what're you talking about? Are you going to burn some *moxa* on Ken's soul?"

"Of course not, silly child."

"What then?"

"The old man," she said excitedly. "Mr. Oka will be our counterirritant. I'm going to have a talk with him tomorrow."

"What are you talking about, Grandma Kurihara?"

But the old woman sank down again in her cot and drew the covers up to her chin. She uttered a great long sigh and began to murmur her prayers. Long before she was finished both Emi and Yuki were sound asleep.

16

KEN SAT OUTSIDE IN BACK OF THE GROCERY STORE, LETTING the sun warm his body and comfort his leg. He leaned against the building, his eyes closed, and he tried to shut out the sounds that grated against every nerve. He couldn't stand the noise. He hated hearing the buses going by in front of the store, and he shouted at Yuki when she turned the radio up too loud. And when there were too many people talking in a room, he simply had to get up and leave.

He gritted his teeth now as he heard someone come out the back door. It was Mr. Oka, but he took care not to slam the door. He lowered himself to the ground beside Ken muttering something about his aching bones.

"I could use a little sunning too," he said quietly.

Ken nodded, his eyes still closed. But he couldn't ignore Hokusai who leaped lightly onto his lap.

"You know your sister threw a pillow at him the first time she saw him."

Ken smiled. "Sounds like Yuki. She never did like cats."

"How about you?"

"Oh I don't mind them. They're quiet. They come greet you occasionally, but then they go off and leave you alone."

The old man nodded. "Exactly right. That's exactly why I like having a cat for a pet. Hokusai's good company."

He offered Ken a cigarette and they sat smoking together. It was good. They weren't saying anything to each other, but the old man knew they were having a good kind of conversation anyway. They understood each other.

The next time the old man had a smoke with Ken out in the sun, he began another kind of conversation. He spoke carefully, knowing what he must do.

"You never should have gone, you know," he began.

"Where?"

"To join the army. Why did you have to be such a hero?"

Ken took a deep breath and looked hard at Mr. Oka. He knew this was a man who needed to hear the truth spoken clearly.

"I guess I went to prove we were just as good as anybody else . . . so kids like Yuki could come back to California and not be ashamed of being Japanese. And . . . well . . . I guess I believed in this country."

117

Ken felt foolish. He didn't like giving speeches even to one old man. He stopped talking.

Mr. Oka leaned closer to Ken and prodded further. "And did you accomplish all that? Did it do any good for you to go and get your leg blasted so you might spend the rest of your life being crippled? You know the world hasn't changed that much in spite of what you did. Isn't that what's churning at your insides now?"

Ken was silent for a moment. "Maybe that's part of it," he said grimly. "But that's not the worst of it. The worst is knowing that Jim's dead and I'm alive."

"But that's war, Kenichi. You were just lucky."

Ken sank back as though the breath had been knocked out of him. "It wasn't just luck. It was because Jim had to be a hero. He threw himself on a grenade to save the rest of us in the shell crater. I could have done it too, but I didn't. If I'd done it, I'd be the one buried over there in that foreign soil and Jim would be back here feeling the sun and smelling the grass."

Ken was crying now, without making a sound. "Damn, stupid, stinking war!"

Mr. Oka sighed. So that was it. Ken couldn't forgive himself because his best friend had died for him.

The old man knew what it was not to be able to forgive. The first week he was in America, lonely and friendless, he had been spat upon by a man in the street. And in all the years after, he had been denied the kind of life any man with white skin could have. So he had harbored a core of resentment that he had nurtured carefully through the years. And he told himself that

118

one day when he had saved enough money, he would return to Japan where he would be as good as any other man walking the streets.

But the war had changed all his plans. He was still in America, beginning all over again, and he was too old and too tired now to go back to Japan. Why then was he still nurturing his hate?

He touched Ken's arm. "I understand your pain, Kenichi," he said.

He wanted to tell Ken it was time to forgive himself, but he didn't know how. So instead he went inside and told Ken's mother and father what they needed to know, so they could understand how it was with their son.

And when Papa heard, he knew what words he had to speak to Ken one day when the time was right and when Ken would listen.

When Grandma Kurihara heard, she brewed a pot of persimmon-leaf tea for Uncle Oka.

"Old man," she said with a slow smile, "you did your work well."

17

THE SHORT DAYS SLIPPED QUICKLY NOW INTO LONG COLD
nights, and the maple leaves turned brown and fluttered
to the ground with the chill winds that blew in from
the bay.

Yuki and Emi had been going to Westview Junior
High for almost two months now and nothing terrible
had happened. Some people in class talked to them and
some didn't, but Yuki could accept that because she
knew that was just how things were going to be.

The worry about Ken continued like a dull ache
for everybody. It was there and it didn't go away and
no one could do anything about it. Ken didn't want to
talk to anyone. And he wouldn't listen to anybody, not
Mama or Papa or Uncle Oka or even the Reverend
Wada who came many times to talk to him.

"Just leave me alone, will you please?" he'd say.

So they simply had to wait. But Yuki was used to waiting. She'd waited for so many things since the war, and now the end of the waiting seemed almost in sight. She hoped it would just be a short wait until Ken was his old self again, and Papa could find a real house for them that they could call home.

Ken, too, seemed to be waiting for something without knowing what that something was. He refused to go and register at the university. He hardly ever went out, and he didn't see any of his old friends who'd come back to Berkeley. Mostly he stayed at home, just sitting and waiting.

Now it was almost Thanksgiving, and there was a kind of stirring in Yuki's blood, a feeling of expectation that seemed stronger this year than ever before. This would be the first Thanksgiving since they were in camp that they could all be together as a family.

"We have so much to be thankful for," Mama said. "The war is over. We're back in California, and Kenichi is home."

She named her private blessings one by one, as though by saying them aloud they became more real to her.

"And we're invited to the Olssens for Thanksgiving dinner," Yuki reminded her.

That seemed like a very good blessing as far as Yuki was concerned. Mrs. Jamieson was invited too, and even Uncle Oka had agreed at last to go with them.

They trooped next door for Thanksgiving dinner looking like a small procession. Papa carried a pot of gold chrysanthemums, Mama took a pumpkin pie she'd baked, Grandma Kurihara took a jar of strawberry jam, and Mrs. Jamieson, looking glorious in an orange cape that almost matched her flaming hair, carried the biggest chocolate cake she'd ever baked. Uncle Oka took some cans of peaches and pears from the shop, and Yuki and Emi folded dozens of gold and red paper cranes to decorate the table.

"I guess I'm the only one to come empty handed," Ken apologized as he greeted Emma Olssen.

"But you brought yourself, Ken," she answered warmly, "and that means more to me today than anything else."

Yuki wondered why there were tears in her eyes when she spoke to Ken.

Ken walked over to the mantel and looked at the large silver frame containing the photograph of a young man.

"That's our Johnny," Stephen Olssen explained. "Just about your age, I imagine, Ken."

"Oh? Where is he now? Still in the service?"

Mr. Olssen glanced at his wife and Yuki saw her nod slightly. "It's all right, Stephen," she said softly. "You can tell them now."

"Our son was killed in Iwo Jima," he said in a voice so low Yuki could scarcely hear.

Mama gasped. "Your only son was killed by the Japanese?" It could have been the son of one of her friends in Japan who had thrown the grenade or pulled the trigger or thrust the bayonet that had killed Johnny Olssen.

"Oh, Mrs. Olssen, I am so very sorry," Mama murmured.

She took Emma Olssen's hands in both of hers, trying to give something of herself to the mother who had lost her son.

Everyone tried to say something comforting. But Ken and Uncle Oka said nothing. It was as though they could find no words to say what they were feeling inside.

Yuki shivered as she felt the close sweep of death once more. And, suddenly, she was so glad Ken was alive and breathing and sitting right there that she got up, stepped carefully over his crutches and lame leg and squeezed herself into the armchair next to him.

"Move over, Ken," she said with a friendly shove. "I want to sit next to you."

"Sure," Ken answered. Yuki felt his arm slip lightly around her shoulder and she knew then that the glass cage was no longer there.

Yuki couldn't remember when she'd eaten such a wonderful dinner. The roast turkey that Emma Olssen carried in from the kitchen, plump and brown and glistening on its bed of parsley, was the biggest turkey she'd ever seen. And with it came candied sweet potatoes, string beans and carrots, and a beautiful cranberry salad molded into a fruit-filled star.

There was such a good feeling of closeness and sharing as they sat together around the big table that Yuki didn't want the day ever to end. She watched Uncle Oka especially. He drank glass after glass of the wine that Stephen Olssen poured for him. And soon, his

face flushed and glistening, he began to talk. He told Mr. Olssen all about his life in America and of the terrible loneliness and anger that had filled it.

Stephen Olssen nodded and listened. "You've had cause for anger, Mr. Oka," he said at last. "But try now to forgive us if you can. Don't destroy yourself with any more bitterness."

The old man looked startled. "Forgive you?" he asked.

"Yes, all of us . . . if you can."

"Can you forgive the soldier who killed your only son?"

"I have already."

Mr. Oka shook his head. "Forgive . . ." he murmured. The word came slowly and softly from his lips, as though he were understanding it for the first time. He spoke the word as a blind man might feel a new object, touching it, discovering it, wondering about it, amazed at the feelings that came alive as he said the word.

Then he said slowly, "I guess forgiving does take the bundle of hate off your back. Still, when you've been wronged for so many years . . ." Mr. Oka paused. "Well, maybe there are ways to fight back without destroying yourself."

Then he glanced at Ken and a certain look passed between them. "I suppose we need to forgive ourselves, just as much as other people," he said.

But Ken said nothing.

No one had missed the words that Mr. Oka spoke, and Grandma Kurihara leaned toward him now saying,

"Well, old man, maybe there is some hope for you after all."

Emi poked Yuki. "Did you hear?" That was the nicest thing she'd ever heard her grandma say to Mr. Oka.

But Yuki was watching Ken. She knew he was listening and thinking. What about Ken, she wondered. Was there hope for him too?

18

LATE THAT NIGHT, AFTER UNCLE OKA HAD RETURNED TO the hostel and Grandma Kurihara and Emi had already gone to bed, Yuki sat with Mama and Papa and Ken in the living room. And she wouldn't go to bed because she couldn't bear to let go of the wonderful warm feeling she'd brought home from next door. If she went to sleep, it would drift away from her during the night and maybe never come back again. She wanted to hold onto the last of today just a little longer, just as she'd clung to Mrs. Jamieson and asked her not to go home.

But Mrs. Jamieson had put on her cape and hat and said firmly, "Yuki, my dear, you must let me go. Old Salt and Felicity and Marigold are at home waiting to be fed. Besides, you don't need me in order to hold onto your joy.

It was hard for Yuki to let go of the people she

loved. She wanted them always to be near and close. She wanted them to close ranks around her, to keep her own small world safe and secure. She moved next to Ken on the sofa now, sitting as close as she could, feeling the fuzz of his sweater rub against her arm.

Mama's hands were folding some laundry, but she had a far off look, as though she were writing some poems in her head. Soon Yuki saw her put down the laundry and go pick up a notebook from the desk. She opened it and began to write, and Yuki saw that for once she wasn't scribbling on a margin or a scrap, she was writing on a fresh, clean piece of paper. It was as though she were finally freeing her poems from the fringes of her life and maybe freeing herself as well.

Papa was reading a newspaper, but Yuki saw him glance at Mama and see what she was doing. A smile of pleasure flickered across his face, but he was careful to hide it with his newspaper so Mama wouldn't stop what she was doing.

Ken sat silent, doing nothing, just staring and maybe thinking. Suddenly, as though he were answering a question someone had just asked, he said, "I might just go back East to finish college. Maybe I could even try for Harvard Medical School someday."

Mama and Papa quickly stopped what they were doing and exchanged a glance filled with their own private happiness.

It was Yuki who spoke first. "You mean you'd leave again?" she asked. "But you just came home. You just finally came back. Why can't you stay and go to school here?"

But Ken wasn't listening. It was almost as though he were straining to be free of the chair and his lame leg and this room and everything that held him here. And he was looking at Papa, not Yuki.

Papa had been waiting a long time to talk to Ken, and he knew now that Ken was ready at last to listen to the words he'd been wanting to say.

"Ken, you're a survivor, just as we all are—your mama, Mr. Oka, Grandma Kurihara and I. We're survivors from another land—the land of your samurai grandfathers. Their strength was our strength as we struggled to make new lives for ourselves in America. Make it your strength too, Ken. Hold on to it and be strong."

Papa stood up now and began to pace up and down. "Your friend lost his life, but you *have* life, Ken. You survived! Don't hate yourself for that. Just accept it. The way I see it, I think what you owe Jim Hirai and Johnny Olssen is life itself. You have an obligation to cherish this precious thing you have. Am I making sense?"

Papa stopped suddenly, as though he felt he'd said too much. "You'll make a fine doctor, Ken. I know you will."

Mama was nodding all the time Papa spoke, as though she were saying every word of it to Ken herself as well. She used the corner of a pillowcase on her lap to wipe her eyes.

"Oh, Kenichi," she said, "we'd be so proud of you."

Ken looked a little embarrassed. He pulled at his lame leg and looked at it a long time, as though he were studying every bone and muscle in it that he couldn't see.

"Well, I can still use my hands," he said slowly.

"Of course you can," Papa agreed. "And there's nothing wrong with your head, either."

"If he's got any brains left up there," Yuki heard herself say. And suddenly, she reached over and poked Ken in the ribs.

Ken turned and grinned at her. Then he reached out and gripped the back of her neck just the way he used to do.

"Okay, Yuki, that's enough out of you." He pushed her up off the sofa. "Get going, now. It's time you went to bed."

"Okay, okay, I'm going, I'm going."

And in that very instant, Yuki knew that the old Ken had come back at last. Everything had somehow fallen into place inside his head. And the curious thing was that almost at the same moment, everything inside her own head had come together too. She knew now that it was all right for Ken to want to leave. He needed to be free, and the reason he could free himself now was because he'd really come home at last.

Yuki went to her room and heard Grandma Kurihara and Emi making the soft, steady sounds of sleep. She looked at Emi and knew she was a survivor too. All she had in this world was this room and two suitcases and her grandma. But that was all she wanted. She wasn't waiting for anything.

And Yuki knew now that she was going to stop waiting, too. She groped her way to the bureau and opened the top drawer. Rummaging about, feeling with her fingers what she couldn't see, she found the small black velvet box with the ring Mrs. Jamieson had given her. She took it out and slipped it on her finger. Then she sat down on the edge of Emi's bed.

"Hey, Emi, look," she said.

"Huh? What? Is it time to get up?"

Yuki held out her hand so Emi could see the creamy white pearl that seemed to glow even in the darkness. "Look what I got out," she said. "I'm going to wear it to church Sunday."

Emi stretched, yawning. "Honest? How come? I thought you were saving it for when you could really celebrate moving into a house of your own."

Yuki shrugged. "I changed my mind," she said. "I'm not going to keep waiting any more. I decided I'm home right now."

Emi grinned. "Well, it's about time," she said. And she flopped over on her side and went back to sleep.

Yuki crept into her bed but she couldn't sleep. She looked around at the familiar dark shapes around her and felt safe and secure. She tried to think of some mental messages to send to somebody, but there were no more messages to send. Everyone she cared about was here with her now. They'd all come home at last, even Ken. And Yuki knew that everything was going to be all right. She'd finally come home too.